MIS

MISSING

A Finn Delaney New York City Mystery

Book 1

Robert L. Bryan

First Edition

Amazon Digital Services LLC

For Meghan and Cuddles – Together Again

Contents

Thank you for purchasing MISSING, the first book in the Finn Delaney New York City Mystery series. If you enjoyed reading about the adventures of Finn and company I would encourage you to take a look at the books in the rest of the series.   Thanks again for your support - Bob

Book 2: THE DEMON WITHIN

https://www.amazon.com/dp/B07TBC1XYQ

Book 3: THE SECURITY SCHOOL

https://www.amazon.com/dp/B0844SKKST

Book 4: DEFUNDED

https://www.amazon.com/dp/B08F2XBRRS

Book 5: THE CARD

https://www.amazon.com/dp/B08R989X26

THE PHOTOGRAPH

The photo was housed in a cheap plastic frame hung prominently on the living room wall in the same Middle Village, Queens, New York City home for over thirty years. The frame obscured the date June 30, 1986 printed on the rear of the 8 x 10 photo. The picture was simple yet provided a complete historical account of an American family. Four subjects, three attired in New York City Police Department uniforms, stood straight and proud. On the left was eighty-eight-year-old retired First Grade Detective Finbar Seamus Delaney, remarkably vibrant looking in a dark suit, full head of silver hair, with the posture of a Marine. Finbar had been a detective during the wild and colorful era of the Roaring Twenties and prohibition. Finbar's son, Lieutenant Patrick Michael Delaney was next. Those who knew the intimacies of the photo understood the image would be the last time Patrick Michael would wear his uniform. Lieutenant Delaney would turn sixty-three, the NYPD's mandatory retirement age, two weeks after the photo was taken. Sergeant Patrick Sean Delaney was next in line. Patrick Sean also put his uniform in storage after the posed photo, but for a different reason than his father. Under a magnified view of the picture, the Detective Bureau's DB collar brass was visible on Sergeant Delaney's dress uniform, and he would be returning to his work in the 5th Precinct PDU, or Precinct Detective Unit, where no uniform was required. On the right end of the line was Patrick James Delaney. Patrick James was unable to maintain the stoic look of his father, grandfather, and great grandfather. A wide grin covered the face of the rookie resplendent in his brand-new NYPD uniform on his graduation day.

Deputy Chief Patrick James Delaney surpassed all his ancestors in NYPD achievements, both in rank and commendations. Throughout the years, the photograph served as a source of inspiration. Whenever the Chief was experiencing a sullen moment, he would study the photo and think about how the next generation of Delaney's would take the baton and surpass his achievements. Of late, however, the photo had brought out the opposite effect. It had become so painful for the Chief to view the picture that he actually considered taking it off the wall – but he just couldn't do it.

CAREER CHANGE

APRIL 28th - Finbar Delaney paused one more time. He scanned his room and his brain to ensure he wasn't forgetting anything. He wanted to get the day's proceedings over with, and he had no desire to return for round two because he had forgotten to bring some essential document with him.

Finn carefully walked down the stairs, the cautious nature of his steps at this point an instinctual act to protect his right knee. He paused and gazed at the photograph. He completely ignored a relatively new photo of him with his father, and instead focused on the four generations of Delaney's. Finn harbored little resentment regarding his situation but figured if he needed to be bitter about anything, let his focus be on something more primal. Finn always hated his name. Thank goodness when he was fourteen a major shoe manufacturer came out with a line of sneakers known as Finns. The sneaker's logo was a shark's fin with "FINN" printed inside the shape. Billboards, baseball caps, and T-shirts of the "Shark Finn" logo exploded everywhere, and suddenly there was a degree of coolness to his name – his nickname, that is. To this day, Finn still hated being called "Finbar."

His father's explanation of honoring his great grandfather, and Finn's great-great grandfather made no sense. If it was so important to pay homage to great-great grandpappy Delaney, Finn was staring at three other prime candidates for the name who somehow managed to avoid the "Finbar" moniker.

The eight-mile trip via New York City bus and subway took over an hour. Finn paused at the top of the steps. It was time to regroup before continuing his journey. Nine months earlier it would have been laughable to think that a subway ride from Queens to Manhattan would require such effort.

Manhattan's Municipal Building enveloped an entrance to New York City's oldest subway station, with columns and an ornately tiled vaulted ceiling hiding the sunlight. Adequately rested, Finn squinted as he departed the sanctuary of the Municipal Building and strode onto the sun-drenched concourse of NYPD Police Headquarters. His strides were deliberate and measured, and he hoped they looked natural. It had been only a week since he stopped using a cane and he was very self-conscious about walking with a noticeable limp. He kept trying to convince himself that slow and steady wins the race as he methodically made his way towards the high security entrance to One Police Plaza while trying to stay out of the way of the bulk of pedestrian traffic moving at a much faster pace.

A string of metal barriers funneled the masses toward the security house located just outside 1PP. The uniformed police officer at the open window sat emotionless, eyes darting from one shield and ID card to the next. Finn already had the black leather wallet in his left hand as he unconsciously guided his right across the barrier's top railing for support. The cop maintained his non-emotional demeanor at the sight of Finn's shield and ID card. Finn did not return his wallet to his pocket, but instead kept it in his left hand as he pushed through the revolving doors. Once inside the building, he placed his ID card against the pedestal. The green light and clicking sound provided evidence that it was ok to push through the turnstile.

The elevator ride to the 9th floor presented ample opportunity to return the wallet to his rear pants pocket. Finn had not been inside headquarters since Zero Day at the academy, when his recruit company visited the Equipment Section on the first floor to pick up uniform items. He roamed the 9th floor like any other person who had never been to the location, scanning room numbers as he got closer and closer to his destination. Finally, the number 922 became visible above the open door. He walked through the doorway and stood in front of a very disinterested looking female who sat behind a large, worn, industrial metal desk. The female did not acknowledge Finn's presence as she twirled her long blond hair with her right index finger and paged through the NY Daily News with her left hand. 25-year old Police Officer Finbar Delaney cleared his throat and stated his business. "I'm here to retire, ma'am."

Some people say that at the moment of death, your entire life flashes before your eyes. For Finn Delaney, a similar phenomenon occurred as he sat quietly listening to the sporadic taps on the keyboard. The police administrative aide preparing Finn's retirement paperwork possessed virtually no typing skills, resulting in ample time for reflection.

The first image to appear in Finn's mind was his father. From the moment Finn could understand the significance of the photograph in his living room, he knew that the New York City Police Department was a Delaney family tradition. In fact, Finn never recalled ever being asked about his career aspirations. It was just assumed that Finn would follow in his father's and all the other Delaney's footsteps. The cerebral scene switched to the morning a year and a half earlier when Finn received the phone call from the Applicant Investigation Unit directing him to report two days later for appointment as a police officer. The look of pride on his father's face was an especially vivid image. Just as vivid was his dad's same proud look as they posed together in full dress uniform at Madison Square Garden after the graduation ceremony, the same photograph that now shared the spotlight with the other living room wall photo.

The flashbacks transitioned to audio as Finn heard his father's words resonating over and over again.

"While you are on probation, Finn, you have to walk on egg shells. Almost anything can get you fired. And if you get hurt off duty, there's no three quarters, and probably no pension at all while you're a probie."

Deep down Finn knew his father was just giving him the good advice any father would provide his son. The probation period was a sensitive time for a young police officer. While on probation, a cop had no right to a department hearing and could be terminated for no reason at the discretion of the police commissioner. Injuries were also a probationary concern. Normally, if a cop was injured while on duty and the injury was severe enough to prevent him/her from performing the job of a full duty police officer, the cop could be granted a line of duty disability pension. This was commonly referred to as three quarters because the cop received three quarters of his salary tax free. If the injury was sustained off duty, the cop would receive an ordinary disability pension, or taxable half pay. An off-duty injury while on probation could very well result in no pension at all. The volume in Finn's mind suddenly turned to the loudest level as he recalled his father's warning.

"Don't be stupid. Give up the hockey until you complete probation!"

Visual flashbacks again took control as Finn flew down the right wing, accelerating to the right as he stick-handled past the back skating defenseman. He was past the defense and moving on the goal. All the forces in nature were converging. The two pursuing defensemen, Finn, and the goalie all came together at the goal. That Finn's mental imagery would go blank was understandable. When all the bodies crashed together into the steel goalpost, he had lost all connection to his senses, except one – pain! Finn had no conscious recollection to replay exactly how his knee was shattered, but the result was certain. As if responding to a mental fast forward button, Finn could now see and hear the doctor telling him that after the surgery his knee would heal to the point that he would be able to resume normal life activities, but that he would no longer be able to perform the duties of a police officer. Etched in Finn's brain was the look on his father's face. It was a very complicated look – a combination of anger, empathy, sadness, and helplessness – helpless at not being able to pull any strings to keep Finn on the job. The best Chief Delaney could do was keep Finn from being outright terminated. Due to his off-duty knee injury, he was awarded an ordinary medical disability pension.

"You're all set."

The words of the inept typist snapped Finn out of his trance. She handed him a folder containing copies of all his retirement paperwork.

"Congratulations and good luck."

The typist was already walking away before Finn could consider whether it was appropriate for her to offer him congratulations.

Right around $30 thousand a year. That's what Finn would receive for a one-and-a-half- year career with the NYPD. Finn had yet to decide if his glass was half empty or half full. On one hand, he had many friends who would jump at the opportunity to sit home and do nothing while collecting 30K annually, but he couldn't help but consider the reality of the half empty option. Thirty years from now, what was his thirty grand a year going to be worth? The reality facing Finn Delaney as he exited police headquarters as a 25- year old retired member of the service was that he was going to have to do something with his life – but what?

MAY 1st - The running track was moderately peppered with joggers and walkers of varying ages and fitness levels. The Spanish shouts and cheering resonating from the soccer match in the field inside the track made the entire area seem much more congested than it really was.

Finn hated walking around a track. He would much rather walk around the perimeter of Juniper Park, but the hard surface of the concrete sidewalk was not good for the rehabilitation of his knee. But the exercise was necessary, and as boring and mundane as it was, the doctor warned him to walk on a track, with its softer surface providing a much better cushion for his knee. With his slow, measured pace, Finn practiced proper track etiquette by staying in the outside lane.

This day's walk was a little different with the adjacent lane occupied by his father. As they walked side by side the contrast in physical appearance could not be missed. Patrick Delaney was a hulk of a man – 6' 3" tall, broad shouldered and barrel chested. Finn, on the other hand, was 5'9" and slim. Both Delaney men shared an athletic inclination, but Patrick had starred as an offensive lineman on his high school and college football teams, while Finn's lean build provided evidence of his forays into track, baseball, and tennis. Oh yes. Finn also loved to play hockey.

Finn's sudden retirement status had not created a financial crisis. He was living in his parents Middle Village home before the injury and had no plans to leave. His disability pension was more than enough to keep him going for the immediate future.

"So, what are your plans Fineous?" Patrick addressed Finn by a nickname he started calling him for no particular reason at age three. Finn hesitated a moment to allow the cheers from the nearby soccer goal to die down.

"Well, I guess I'll go home and take a shower."

"Don't be a smart ass. You know what I mean. Going forward. What do you plan to do?"

Finn looked down at the track, noting that he had drifted onto the right edge of the marked lane. "I don't really know," he said, keeping his eyes fixed on the track below him.

"Isn't there anything that interests you?"

"Not really." Finn felt very bad for providing that response, but it was true. He really did not have any interest in another profession, and why should he. He never had any great passion to be a police officer, but ever since he could walk the mantra he heard from his dad was "be a cop – be a cop." So, he became a cop, and now he could no longer be a cop. It wasn't his fault that he had no other career aspirations, was it? What was he supposed to do now with his useless degree in criminal justice? He couldn't practice law or medicine, and no one was lining up to hire him as an architect or engineer. He really wished his father would face the truth. He had been groomed to be one thing and one thing only in life – a cop.

Finn was ready for a fight. He was sure his dad was about to tear into him with accusations of laziness and lack of focus. He was therefore quite surprised with what his father had to say.

"If you don't know what you want to do, I may have an idea for you."

As they navigated one of the track's long turns, Finn adjusted his stare from the track to his father.

"What?"

"Private Detective."

Finn's response was the same. "What?"

"You heard me Fineous." Patrick sounded very upbeat as he explained. "You can become a licensed New York State Private Investigator. This way you can stay in the law enforcement field – somewhat."

The accentuation of the word "somewhat" was not lost on Finn. Patrick Delaney came from a world where you were either NYPD or you were nothing. Still, his dad was trying to point him in some direction, and he appreciated the effort. He would hear him out without interruption.

"I have the study materials for you to go over before you take the test. It's not that hard. You should have no problem passing."

Finn had no desire to rain on his dad's parade, but he believed he had to point out an obstacle to his plan. "Isn't there an experience requirement to be licensed as a PI?"

"There is, but that requirement is waived for retired police officers."

Finn's voice took on an incredulous tone. "It's waived for retired officers with twenty years on the job, right? Not retired cops who never got off probation."

Patrick put his massive right arm around Finn's shoulder and pulled him close for a hug.
"Trust me, that's not going to be an issue."

Finn understood immediately. Obviously, his father had finally found a string he could pull, probably someone at the New York State Department of State who would take a very liberal view of his police experience. Patrick interpreted Finn's silence as acquiescence with his plan. "If you're going to do this, I want you to do it right. I'll provide the start up financing for your business. We'll get you set up in an office and we'll come up with an advertising and marketing plan. I'll even hire a secretary for you."

They had left the track and were two blocks from home when Finn voiced his final concern. "There's only one small problem. I don't know anything about being a private detective."

Patrick remained upbeat. "That's ok. You didn't know anything about being a cop, did you?"

THE OFFICE

JUNE 15th - The aroma from the Spanish chicken take out joint downstairs was strong. The office was painted a very faded shade of yellow, with chipping and stains dominating all sides. Two very dirty and old casement style windows faced Woodhaven Boulevard. On one of the two grey desks sat a desktop computer, a notebook lying open, and a stack of papers sitting under a turtle-shaped paperweight. Who these items belonged to was a mystery. Finn smiled. Perhaps this was his first case.

In a corner, the air conditioner was blasting at medium, and there was a swivel chair in the middle of the office. A bookshelf, bursting with books was in a corner, with yet another stack of papers under a paperweight that was shaped to look like a skunk. The books communicated a professional image, but a closer inspection revealed a set of 1970s encyclopedias along with an assortment of high school text books and cook books. Finn walked to the center of the room and made a slow 360-degree turn, taking in every ounce of atmosphere. He placed his hands on his hips and shook his head. This was without doubt the worst looking office he had ever seen.

The sounds of heavy steps getting progressively louder indicated an arrival from the stairs. Finn's dad had returned to his car to retrieve something important. Finn took a deep breath and tried to maintain a positive attitude for his father's sake.

"Pretty sweet, huh?" Patrick said while crossing towards the windows.

"Yeah. Great." Finn was making a concerted effort to sound sincere.

Patrick was holding something in a bag. Finn had no idea what the bag was obscuring, but he could tell it was about two feet by three feet and flat. A wide smile appeared on Patrick's face as he began to make the big reveal. Finn was speechless, but not in a good way. Patrick held up a sign for Finn to view. He apparently had the sign professionally made, with FINBAR DELANEY running across the top of the sign in an arc, and PRIVATE DETECTIVE arcing across the bottom of the sign. If name and title was the only information contained on the sign, Finn could have lived with it. Dominating the center of the sign, however, was a ridiculous looking eyeball. Finn laughed only because it was a better alternative to crying.

"Oh boy! Finbar Devine – private eye – wow!"

The proud father mounted the sign in the window and immediately ran down the stairs to see how it looked from the street and to take pictures. There would soon be new photos on the living room wall.

Finn was still frozen in the center of the office when Patrick returned. He immediately hugged Finn. "Good luck Fineous. All the best."

"Thanks dad." Finn's thoughts quickly shifted to how quickly he could cover that sign after his father had departed.

Finn thought he heard sounds on the stairs, but when no one appeared in the office he figured he had simply heard activity emanating from the street or the Spanish chicken place. A few minutes later, however, additional sounds distracted him from his father's conversation. His initial instincts had been correct as evidenced by the emergence of a figure from the stairway. Finn audibly gasped. The woman before him, who had taken about five minutes to make it up the stairs, had to be a minimum of eighty years old. She was very short and frail with wide, horned rimmed glasses, and she had a big head of hair that resembled a white version of a fright wig. A cane in her right hand helped her to slowly navigate the floor while a small brown bag remained tightly secured in her left hand.

"Whew! I'm going to have to remember to bring my lunch from now on. I don't want to do these stairs more than once a day."

Patrick walked to the old woman and placed his hand on her shoulder. "Fineous, this is Gladys Kowalski – your secretary."

Finn remained silent. This day was chock full of one stunning moment after the other. For some reason, only one thought entered his mind. Who the hell was named Gladys? As quickly as his mind had asked the question it supplied an answer. Women over eighty years old are named Gladys, that's who.

Finn smiled and extended his hand to Gladys. "It's a pleasure to meet you." As he gingerly shook her boney hand, his smile widened. It had suddenly occurred to him that Finbar Delaney, private eye, had just broken his first mystery. The mystery of the owner of the papers on the desk was solved. Maybe he was a natural at this game. Oh well, on to the next case.

ACROSS THE STREET

JUNE 30th - Finn fidgeted in a vain attempt to get comfortable. Even with his feet up on the desk, the very old office chair provided almost no support or comfort. He enviously eyed the empty chair behind the only other desk in the office. This was a brand-new chair and appeared to be extremely ergonomic. Maybe he should just switch chairs. After all, he was the boss of this enterprise, wasn't he?

It was 9:30 AM and the new comfortable chair should have been occupied for thirty minutes. During the existence of Delaney Investigations Inc., however, Finn had become accustomed to Gladys Kowalski gasping for breath while emerging from the stairs any time between 9:30 and 10:00. Finn planted his feet firmly on the floor and began to rise from his ancient chair. He stopped before reaching a fully standing position and re-planted his butt in the chair. He repeated this action three times before facing the reality that even the boss could not take the good chair away from a frail, 83-year-old woman. Maybe he should just ask his dad to buy another chair. Finn shook his head. He couldn't do that either. This entire operation had not cost Finn one dime. His father had set up everything – the office, the computers, Finn's private investigator license, incorporating the business, a marketing plan, the ridiculous sign in the window, and even Gladys. How much of an ingrate would he be to now ask for a new chair?

At 9:45 Finn began hearing noises coming from the stairwell. These noises had quickly become a familiar signal. Gladys had begun her trek up the stairs and would enter the office in five to ten minutes. At 9:55 the familiar scene unfolded. Gladys shuffled across the office, her cane in her right hand tapping the floor as she slowly navigated, and a brown breakfast bag clutched tightly in her left hand.

"Good morning, Gladys."

Gladys waited until the huffing and puffing became manageable. "Whew! Did you add some steps to those stairs? Good morning."

Gladys let out a huge sigh of relief as she settled into the comfortable new chair. Another day at the office had begun, and in all likelihood, it would be as uneventful as each preceding day. At least the lack of business activity had given Finn the opportunity to establish some required administrative protocols. He learned while studying for the private investigator licensing test that the New York State Department of State had some very specific regulations regarding how private investigators conducted business. Records had to be maintained in a prescribed manner, including preparing a written contract for every client, regardless of the duration of the case. Finn was able to create templates for all the required documents he would need. Now, if only there would be some business so he could utilize the forms. Finn waited until he was sure Gladys had finished her muffin.

"Any activity on the website overnight?"

"Huh?" Gladys didn't seem to understand that language.

"The website – the computer." Finn kept smiling and maintained his patience.

"Oh yeah. I'm really beginning to get the hang of turning this gizmo on."

Finn rolled his eyes and opened his laptop. His father had set up the website and paid for some online advertising. The website had a contact page where potential clients could request a consultation for an investigation.

"Don't bother, Gladys. I just checked the site. Nothing, as usual."

Gladys was still struggling to find the desktop's "on" button as Finn began to make his exit from the office. "I'll be across the street."

During his limited life experience Finn had always been skilled at accepting the reality of a situation. Whether it was during school, or in his social life he was always able to adapt, accept, and move on. A case in point was Jennifer. Finn met Jen during their junior year at St. John's University and their relationship lasted for just under five years. All of Finn's friends and family just assumed that Finn and Jen would eventually get married. So, when Jen decided that she loved the fireman she had been secretly seeing for six months, everyone was shocked. Everyone except Finn, that is. He made no effort to win Jen back. He simply adapted, accepted, and moved on. Finn reacted much the same way to his forced early retirement from the NYPD. There was nothing he could do about it, so he accepted the status quo and moved on.

His ability to go with the flow made it easy for Finn to take the problems with is new business start-up in stride. So what if he had no clients. His office was all of six blocks from his home, and it provided somewhere for him to go every day. Money was not an issue yet, and he did not have to sit and stare at Gladys all day. He could simply go across the street.

Delaney Investigations Inc. was located on the northwest corner of Woodhaven Blvd. and 65th Street. For the past 35-years the southwest corner had been occupied by The Shamrock. The owners of most modern Irish pubs go to great lengths to create atmosphere. The Shamrock, on the other hand, organically reeked atmosphere. The interior was low, narrow, and dark with the heavy black beams running the length of the ceiling sending a strong signal the pub was very old. The numerous sports photos and paintings on the wall behind the long oak bar along with the assortment of hand painted Gaelic signs on the opposite wall added to the environment. Finn took a seat at the empty bar, immediately discovering the stool to be more comfortable than his office chair. It was only 10:00 AM and the pub didn't officially open until 11:00. His time in the office had provided Finn with the insight that that he could push on the heavy wooden door at 10:00, and instantly find himself swimming in the pub's ambiance. Finn looked around the empty bar in admiration. The atmosphere was better appreciated in the dimly lit quiet. Finn had spent many nights at the Shamrock while it was rocking. It was difficult to appreciate this peaceful atmosphere with the jukebox blaring 80s rock and two young bartenders struggling in vain to keep up with the calls from the two-deep crowd at the bar. Adding to the nightly chaos were the cheers and groans of groups of mostly young men completely focused on a large screen HD television mounted as high on the wall as was possible, which wasn't all that high considering the low ceiling height. Whether it was the Yankees, Mets, Rangers, Islanders, Jets, or Giants, the TV always had a large, boisterous crowd below it.

Finn nodded as he looked around and recognized that this complete state of peace and quiet is what a pub truly should be. He chuckled slightly, however, when he considered how quickly a pub would be out of business if it was always empty.

"What's up my brother?"

The kitchen door swung closed and two fresh cups of coffee were placed on the bar. Finn shook his head in response to the display of a bottle of Bailey's, but the liquor found its way into the other cup.

"Mmm. That's the only way I can drink coffee."

Kevin Malone put the cup back on the bar. One of the unintended consequences of Finn's new career was the ability to spend most of his work day hanging out with his childhood friend. Kevin was the ultimate square peg in a square hole. From the day Finn met him in the first grade Kevin showed zero interest in school work, education in general, or a career. Kevin simply loved to talk and socialize. If ever there was a man cut out to be the day time bartender at the Shamrock, it was Kevin. His 6'5" smiling Irish face under a thick mane of red hair only added to the atmosphere of the pub.

"Any cases yet, bro?"

"Nothing." Finn answered while flipping the pages of the New York Post

Coffee and a newspaper with Kevin had now become the normal course of business for Finn. It certainly beat sitting around all day in the office with Gladys. While Finn perused the Post, Kevin flipped through the Daily News.

"No wonder business in the bar is so good. There's nothing but bad news in the paper." Kevin took another sip of his Irish coffee before elaborating. "The market is down, we're on the verge of war in Asia, and the Yanks lost again." Kevin flipped a page and shook his head.

Here's something positive." Finn pointed to the article as a reference for Kevin. "The King of Bahrain is in the City to announce the opening of ten auto plants in the Southeast and Midwest."

Kevin had begun wiping down the bar with a towel. "Who the hell is the king of brains? Is he supposed to be the smartest guy in the world?"

Finn closed the paper and squinted toward Kevin. "Not brains – it's 'Bah-Rain' – a country in the Middle East. My God, do you ever consider reading a book occasionally?"

Kevin continued working the towel toward the far end of the bar. "I read all the time. A lot more than you think smart ass."

"Wrestling magazines don't count."

The bar towel flew from Kevin's hand, grazing the right side of Finn's face.

"Screw you, Finbar!" Kevin knew that Finn hated being called by his proper name. "And what exactly is so positive about some Arab king opening auto plants in the USA. Jesus, don't we have enough Arabs here?"

"Jobs, my tolerant, progressive friend." Finn tossed the towel back to Kevin. "These new plants are going to produce the BM Mansour."

"The What?"

"It's a new model sports car being manufactured by Bahrainian Motors."

Kevin came out from behind the bar and sat on the stool next to Finn. "What's a Mansour?"

Finn placed his empty coffee cup on the bar. "It's the first name of the king's son – the crown prince of Bahrain. These new plants mean thousands of new jobs for Americans. This may shock you, but there is a world of knowledge at your disposal right here." Finn displayed his iPhone for Kevin's benefit and then began reading from the screen. "For example, since its independence in 1971, Bahrain and the United States have maintained a complicated relationship. Bahrain has provided a base for U.S. naval activity in the Persian Gulf since 1947. When Bahrain became independent the US-Bahrain relationship was formalized with the establishment of diplomatic relations. Even though Bahrain continued to be a reliable ally in a volatile region of the world, the United States had ongoing problems with Bahrain's human rights record." Finn looked up from the screen. "So, you see, someone like you with little regard for human rights might do very well in Bahrain."

Kevin took the bar towel and wrapped it around the top of his head. "Maybe you have something there. I'd fit right in, right?"

"Unbelievable!" Finn put his phone on the bar. "The bottom line is these new plants represent a tremendous financial windfall for Bahrain, especially for the king and the royal family."

"Whatever." Kevin removed his makeshift turban and resumed wiping down the bar. He paused his work for a moment of reflection. "You know something – the king of brains wouldn't be a bad name for a bad guy wrestler."

"Wonderful." Finn gingerly hopped off the stool, putting all his weight on his left leg. "I better go check on Gladys."

"Yeah, she may have died while you were gone."

Finn's exit was short circuited by a voice from the kitchen area.

"How many people are we expecting, Kevin?"

"Twenty-five. Hey, come see who stopped in."

A figure came out of the shadows of the dining room and approached the bar.

"Oh my God, Finn!"

The bubby exclamation came from Meghan Hogan. Finn nearly fell over when he took a step back and tripped on the stool. Along with Kevin, Meg was one of Finn's closest friends growing up. Even though he had never been romantically involved with Meghan, the trio had still hung out regularly right up until Finn started seeing Jen. Jen could never understand the concept of Finn having a female friend, so their connection abruptly ceased. Meghan still lived four blocks from Finn, but he had not talked to her in years. Even after the break up with Jen, Finn felt too guilty to simply try to resume communications as if nothing had ever happened.

Kevin, who had orchestrated this uncomfortable moment, tried to ease the tension. "Meg just started hostessing here at night, but we have a luncheon coming in at twelve."

"That's great," Finn nodded, having absolutely no idea what else to say.

"How's your mom and dad?" Meg inquired.

"They're great." Finn kept nodding and supplying the same answer.

Meghan's smile turned into a frown. "I heard about what happened with the police department. I'm so sorry. How's your knee?"

Finn was still nodding and unable to change his stock answer. "It's great." Finn grimaced slightly in recognition of his ridiculous response.

Finn kept nodding while Meg stood silently watching him nod. Kevin finally ended the epic encounter.

"Uh, I think we better keep getting ready. These people will be here before we know it."

"Oh yeah – you're right. I should get back to the kitchen." Meg took one step but then turned back. "It was great seeing you, Finn."

Finn was still incapable of another response. "Yeah, great."

Meghan disappeared into the kitchen while Kevin gloated in the discomfort he had caused. "What's wrong, bro? Meg still likes you – can't you see that? She's cute and ready for the picking. Are you gonna hit that or what?"

Finn mustered the dirtiest look possible as a response to Kevin's crude declaration. He shook his head as he hit the door. "Later, Kev."

DOWN TO BUSINESS

SEPTEMBER 15th -- Finn was flying on instruments. That's what he called it when he had no idea where he was going and was relying totally on the automated verbal directions from his GPS. Finn found this aspect of life in New York City to be fascinating. He was traveling within the borough where he had lived his entire life, yet, he had the feeling he was in a foreign country.

Whitestone was the northernmost neighborhood in Queens, situated between the Whitestone Bridge and the Throgs Neck Bridge. Its shoreline was largely comprised of upper income tract mansions and high-rise apartments. Finn never thought locating the address would be so complicated. He was very familiar with Utopia Parkway as the major roadway adjacent to his alma mater, St. John's University. As Finn found out, however, Utopia Parkway ran from Saint John's in Jamaica Estates all the way to the tip of Whitestone. When his instruments directed Finn to come in for landing, the location was not like any Utopia Parkway he was familiar with. Finn was slowly drifting along a one lane dead end road bordered by a body of water and the Throgs Neck Bridge.

Based on the identical appearance of the dozen or so high ranch homes lining the waterfront, Finn's deductive mind concluded they were developed at the same time. Finn pulled to the curb in front of 14-12. He wasn't sure if another vehicle could fit past him, but he had no other alternative. Besides, if a vehicle did come down this isolated road they would honk the horn, wouldn't they?

Finn had been out on the road more often lately. Slowly but surely, he began splitting his work day between hanging out at the Shamrock and actual work, but he always made sure Meghan wasn't working before going across the street. His father's marketing campaign was finally beginning to pay off, evidenced by the receipt of some small jobs. Although he was happy to finally get some work, Finn was a little disheartened by the quality of the jobs. He was a licensed private investigator, but the entirety of what he knew about being a PI was from various TV shows, movies, and books. The marketing campaign became a magnet for random people whose lives had become so bad they decided that calling a PI was their last desperate step. The result was a steady stream of income generated from oddball clients with oddball cases. The best of these bad cases involved following and video recording cheating husbands or boyfriends. Not only did Finn find surveillance to be an extremely difficult task, but he also felt a little sleazy about creeping around motel parking lots with a video camera. Moreover, Finn couldn't help but feel he was betraying some primal man-code by spying on the cheaters. Much later, Finn learned that "Real" private investigators never took these so-called domestic cases because they were always a huge mess. These real PIs received almost all their work from lawyers and insurance companies. Until Finn could work his way into the mainstream, however, he would have to be content making his living via his cavalcade of crazies. Some of Finn's more memorable cases during those early days included:

- Being hired to see what a cat was doing while the owner was working. Finn found himself following the cat through a residential neighborhood for three days. His final investigative report to the client divulged that the cat walked around the streets, licked itself, and climbed trees – But the client's check was good.

- In a switch from his usual cheater case, Finn was hired by a husband to follow his wife. On the first night of surveillance, Finn followed the wife to a sleazy Brooklyn motel named "Joey's." He didn't see anyone visit the wife at the motel, so before night two Finn conducted some Internet research. He found some terrible reviews of the motel including one that said the place was mostly run by the owner's son, who was a druggie and would ask people who stayed there if he could buy any prescription drugs they had. Later that evening Finn drove direct to the motel, but he didn't see the wife's car anywhere in the area. In retrospect, Finn had to admit it was a terrible idea, but at the moment, going to the front desk and asking for the wife seemed like the thing to do. Finn's investigative instincts told him that the desk clerk was the owner's son, especially when the clerk asked if Finn had any Percocet for sale. Finn had no pre-planned strategy, so he reacted with wide-eyed shock when the clerk responded to his inquiry by stating that the wife was in room 214, and did Finn want him to call her. Finn basically panicked – said not to call her and bolted from the motel. Finn retreated to his Toyota Corolla in the motel parking lot and paused for several minutes to collect his thoughts. While he was recalibrating his strategy, a dark Cadillac pulled into the adjacent parking space, and an old guy got out of the caddy and began unloading boxes from the trunk. Suddenly, the desk clerk was present talking to the old man. They were literally standing no more than five feet from Finn, but they didn't notice him. Meanwhile, Finn could hear every word of their conversation, which revealed that the old man was the clerk's father and the owner of Joey's. The case was solved when the son told his father that someone had stopped by looking for his

Gumare. The old man called his son an idiot for revealing the presence of the wife and reinstructed his son that the inquiry was likely made by a private detective. A cleaner from the motel joined the group with a question for the son. The cleaner approached from the driver's side of Finn's car, and remarkably, no one noticed Finn sitting behind the wheel even though the conversation was being conducted across the hood of his vehicle. Finn had all the information he needed, and he didn't know how long his luck would last. The moment the cleaner returned to the motel and the son turned to address his father, Finn pressed the start button, and with the screeching of tires, he was gone. And the check was good.

- Being hired by a client to find out why his dog was getting fat. At least this was an easy case to work. Finn parked across the street from the yard the dog was kept in all day while the owner was at work. This case was solved very easily when Finn observed almost every person who walked by the yard stop to pet and feed the cute little dog. And still, the check was good.
- Being hired by an inmate serving twenty years for manslaughter to find someone to kill the inmate's wife. Finn never found out if that check was good.

Presently, Finn labored up the unusually long set of front steps and rang the doorbell. The initial phone conversation made this case sound very straightforward. Sandra Berkman said her neighbor was harassing her – something about moving her garbage cans. As Finn waited on the stoop he recognized there was something weird about investigating garbage cans, but it didn't seem to be anywhere near the stories of the screwballs he was used to dealing with. He looked around and took in the scenery. The day was windless and warm, yet the strong cool breeze from the bay felt great.

"Hello, Mr. Delaney, I'm Sandra Berkman." The mild mannered, short, plump 60-ish woman seemed exceptionally affable.

"This is quite a view." Finn was following a book on investigations that suggested breaking the ice with a client with small talk before getting into the facts of the case.

"Yes, it is," Sandra responded. She pointed to the right. "Over there is Little Bay Park and this water directly in front of us is Little Bay." Sandra waved in the direction of the bridge. "Across the bay is Fort Totten and behind it is Great Neck." Sandra kept pointing to the bay. "And did you realize that right out there is the point where the East River becomes the Long Island Sound.

"That's amazing." Finn did his best to sound interested.

That facts of Sandra's allegation were a little odd – but seemed simple enough. New York City Sanitation collections picked up on her block on Mondays and Thursdays. She would put her two trash cans at the curb in front of her house early each Sunday and Wednesday evening. Late on those evenings she claimed she would always look out her living room window and see her trash cans knocked over in the street. Sandra was adamant in her assertion that John Dingman, her next-door neighbor for the past thirty years, was coming out late at night and knocking over her cans.

"Have you had any prior problems with Mr. Dingman?"

"No."

"Do you know of any reason he would be knocking over your cans?"

"No."

"Have you ever seen him near your cans?"

"No."

Finn placed his right index finger on his temple. "What makes you think Mr. Dingman is knocking over your trash cans?"

Sandra maintained her pleasant demeanor. "Oh, I know it's him."

"How do you know?"

"Oh, I just know."

Finn didn't know what else to say. He made a mental note to reserve a seat for Sandra Berkman in his growing nut job hall of fame.

Regardless of Sandra's mental state, Finn was there, and he had a very simple suggestion to bring the case to a fast conclusion. Finn introduced technology to his investigative repertoire by mounting an infrared CCTV camera in Sandra's living room window.

SEPTEMBER 16th – Finn did not need his instruments for the return trip to Whitestone. He had to admit to a tinge of excitement at Sandra's call. The trash cans had been knocked over again last night. Finn couldn't wait to review the video from his covert camera.

Again, as Finn waited on the stoop he marveled at the strong cooling winds coming off the bay. Finn plugged the cable from the camera into the USB port on his lap top. Finn nodded. The HD infrared image was sharp. The trash cans stood tall in the middle of the frame. Finn intermittently used fast-forward, but the cans continued to stand. One final fast-forward movement and the cans were down. Finn was excited. He began the gradual rewind process. Rewind a little – still down. Rewind a little more – still down. Rewind more – they're up! Wait a minute. Finn had not seen John Dingman, the creature from the bay, or anyone else for that matter approach those cans when they fell over.

Finn looked out the window to the bay and laughed. What was wrong with him? The answer was so simple. That strong wind off the bay he was so fond of was also the culprit knocking over the trash cans.

Finn was anxious to give Sandra the big reveal. "Sandra," he called out toward the kitchen. "Come here, please. Good news."

Sandra Berkman entered the living room carrying a tray of pastries.

"Yes, Mr. Delaney?" she smiled.

"Mystery solved!" Finn grinned and beckoned Sandra to the lap top. He played the video several times. Finn found Sandra's lack of acknowledgement a bit odd, so he decided he should provide a play-by-play to the video.

“It was the wind!” Finn extended his arms and continued smiling. “That’s all it was. And you do have a very strong wind blowing in off the bay here.”

Sandra remained focused on the screen but said nothing. Finn was perplexed at her lack of response. “I’m sorry, Ms. Berkman, do you understand what I’m saying?”

Sandra sighed deeply and turned toward Finn. “I understand, Mr. Delaney, but unfortunately, this only makes your investigation more difficult.”

Finn shook his head and blinked several times. “I’m sorry Ms. Berkman. I don’t understand.”

Sandra Berman’s right hand slightly rocked up and down while her index finger pointed at the lap top screen. “I think I know how he’s doing it.”

“Doing what?” Finn was lost.

“Dingman, of course.” Sandra was growing more excited by her apparent discovery. “He’s using some type of invisibility field – that’s it!” Sandra spun towards Finn with an excited smile on her face. “How soon can you work on this Mr. Delaney?”

Finn might miss the cool breeze coming off the bay, but as he explained to Sandra Berkman, his caseload commitments were just too busy for him to continue the investigation. He did, however, make a mental note to move Sandra to the front row in his infamous clientele hall of fame. And yet, her check was good

THE PRELIMINARY

SEPTEMBER 23rd - As had become the norm, the message Gladys left on his desk was fragmented and incomplete. As a matter of fact, this message only contained a first name and a phone number – and the phone number didn't even have an area code. Finn settled into his uncomfortable chair and dialed. He would try the local 718 area code first. As he waited for the call to connect, he spoke to himself in anticipation of what he suspected was coming. "OK, Candice – who's cheating on you – boyfriend or husband?"

"Hello." The voice caught Finn off guard. It belonged to an elderly woman, not the typical scorned wife or girlfriend he had become accustomed to dealing with.

"Yes ma'am. This is Finn Delaney the private investigator. What can I do for you?"

Candice Rothchild explained her dilemma. Several months earlier she moved into an apartment building on Queens Blvd. in Forest Hills, and the building superintendent had been harassing her ever since she moved in. When Finn asked for specifics on the harassment, Candice stated that he had placed microphones inside her apartment, and that all night he would pump in the sounds of people talking and music. She said that the noises were driving her crazy and that she could not sleep at night.

During the short drive to Queens Blvd., Finn's instinct to accept the situation came in handy. This old lady would probably turn out to be batshit crazy, but at least it wasn't one of his cheating spouse cases, so he wouldn't have to peek around a corner with a camera.

Parker Towers was a community of four, 20-story upscale apartment buildings located in the middle-class Queens neighborhood of Forest Hills. Candice Rothchild lived on the 16th floor of 67-01 Queens Blvd., the northern-most tower. By the time Finn had been buzzed into the lobby, waited for the painfully slow elevator to come to the lobby, endured the equally slow ride to the 16th floor, and then waited what seemed like an eternity for Candice Rothchild to come to her door, twenty minutes had elapsed. Just as the apartment door was opening, Finn was trying to determine whether the twenty-minute sojourn should be part of his hourly rate.

"Hello young man. Please come in."

Candice Rothchild looked to be at least equal to Gladys's 83 years, but she had a very different look than his secretary. Finn was fishing his mind for a word to best describe Candice. He couldn't decide if distinguished, sophisticated, or classy was the best descriptor. Candice was short and thin, but she was impeccably dressed and groomed, complete with a floral print dress and freshly styled grey hair. Her apartment was equally impressive with a highly polished hardwood floor in a foyer leading to a living room covered by an expensive-looking Persian rug. The décor in the living room was equally upscale with a tan plaid sofa with heavy oak arms, a bookcase neatly stocked with classics, family pictures on one wall, a china cabinet against another, and a beautiful gilded mirror on a third wall. On the final wall, velvet drapes framed the windows, the lace inner curtains drawn, allowing daylight to enter while rendering the majestic view of the Manhattan skyline a blur.

Candice Rothchild certainly didn't sound like a nut. She told her story in a rational, lucid manner. So much so that Finn agreed to return later in the evening and spend the night in the apartment if necessary.

Finn returned to the office around 2 PM. No messages were waiting, and Gladys was AWOL. Nothing new there. As soon as Finn ensured that Gladys was not dead in the bathroom, he decided to go across the street. At this time of the afternoon, Finn would have to share Kevin's attention with four old boozehounds spread out along the bar.

"Hey, it's super-sleuth." Kevin announced as he filled a shot glass for a thirsty customer.

Finn delivered his now standard opening line. "Meg's not here, is she?"

"No, she's not." Kevin responded. "But let me tell you something Finbar. You are really being a grade A jerk!"

Finn scanned the bar visually, unaffected by his friend's verbal barbs. Kevin had decided to leave the Meghan situation alone, and instead focused on the timing of his friend's appearance.

"Here kind of late today. Does that mean we're drinking?" Kevin held up a fresh bottle of Bud. Finn waved off the beer.

"No, I just came from a client. I'm gonna have to go back and spend the night with her."

As the last word rolled past his lips, Finn braced himself for the barrage his poor choice of words would surely bring.

"Well, well. Have we changed occupations to male gigolo?"

"Very funny," Finn stated, reflecting that he had gotten off easy if that was Kevin's only comment. "She happens to be an eighty-three-year-old woman." Finn closed his eyes and bit his lip. After weathering the first storm, another stupid comment had placed himself right back in Kevin's crosshairs.

"Eighty-three, huh! I hope she's paying you well, stud!"

Finn was surprised when Kevin let him off easy for a second time. Kevin was an expert ball breaker, but the reason for his reluctance to fully ply his trade soon became apparent.

"Hey Finn – I saw Tommy Clancy the other day."

"So?" Finn saw nothing special about the sighting of a mutual neighborhood friend.

"So – I know you get along with Tommy, and I was just wondering if you could do me a favor?"

"What?" Finn braced himself. Favors for Kevin were usually not simple.

"Well, I was hoping that you could put in a good word for me for a job with Tommy."

Finn found the request ludicrous, even by Kevin's standards.

"Hey buddy. Isn't this sort of a been there done that situation?"

Kevin remained silent while filling two more glasses as Finn continued the explanation. "The way I remember, you worked for Tommy a couple of years ago."

Their mutual friend, Tommy Clancy was the security manager at Simon's, a very exclusive, high-end Manhattan department store. Kevin had worked as a store detective for a couple of years, and from everything Finn heard, Kevin was very good at the job. Kevin, however, had a knack for ultimately spoiling any good situation, and the end at Simon's occurred when Tommy found him slumped over the next-door bar while he was supposed to be working.

Finn cut directly to the big problem with the favor. 'Tommy's supposed to forget about you getting drunk while you were working?"

Kevin disregarded the request from a boozehound and kept his focus on Finn, shaking his head and maintaining the best sincere look he could muster. "Like I said at the time – everyone got that whole incident wrong. It was a bad reaction to medication. I wasn't feeling good and I went to the bar to get some water to take with my prescription."

Finn had to admire one aspect of Kevin's personality. No matter how big or absurd the lie, his friend committed to it, and he would not break.

"I don't understand why you would even want to work there again?"

"Besides bartending, store detective is what I do best, and let's face it, I need to generate another stream of revenue. How about it, buddy? Anyway, I've changed. I'm much more mature."

Finn almost fell off the stool. "Mature?" Finn stopped himself from saying anything further on the maturity topic and shook his head. "What they hell. I know I'm gonna regret this, but I'll talk to him."

"That's my pal!" Kevin tried to reward Finn with a beer, but again he declined.

The new entry to the pub sang out a greeting while passing the bar.

"Hi Kevin."

There was a moment of silence while both the new entry and Finn recognized each other. Kevin broke the uncomfortable silence.

"Hi Meg. Look who's here?"

Finn shot daggers at Kevin before turning to face Meghan.

"Oh, Hi Finn. Good to see you."

"Same here Meg."

The uncomfortableness returned until Meg provided closure.

"Well, I better get to work. See ya," she concluded before disappearing behind the kitchen doors.

"Yeah. See ya," Finn repeated before spinning on the stool to face Kevin.

"You lying bastard! You told me she wasn't working."

Kevin wagged a finger, a very self-satisfied look on his face.

"Tut, tut, Finbar. You asked me if she was here, and she wasn't. You never asked anything about whether she would be coming here. And while we're on the topic, when are you ever going to ask that poor girl out?"

"You're still an asshole!" were Finn's parting words.

Finn sat on the sofa in the dark living room, surfing the web on his iPhone. This was going to be a long night, but if it made the old lady feel better, he reasoned his stakeout had value. By 3 AM Finn was losing the fight. His iPhone slipped out of his hand to the sofa cushion and his head had become too heavy to support. Slowly his head sagged to the left until it finally came to rest on the sofa's arm. Just as blissful sleep was beginning to set in, something stirred Finn to consciousness. He shot to an upright sitting position and waited the required time for the haze to clear allowing him to finally grasp where he was and what he was doing.

What was that? It sounded like it was coming from the kitchen. With no tactics in mind Finn rushed through the kitchen door and stopped in the middle of the floor. The only sound punctuating the silence was his heavy breathing. He turned on the light and scanned the room. Finn scratched his head. There was absolutely nothing out of place. Was he going crazy too? Finn was retreating back through the kitchen door when he stopped in his tracks. There was that sound again. He spun around and re-entered the kitchen. This time there was more substance to the sound. Was that the sound of a bell? And voices. He couldn't make out the words, but he was definitely hearing voices. But from where? Before the room fell silent again, Finn also heard some type of rumbling sound – like a machine at work. Finn placed a chair directly in the middle of the room and sat down. Then, he waited.

Approximately twenty minutes passed before Finn was shocked to attention by the distinct sound of two bells. Again, there was someone talking but he could still not make out the words, and there was that damn machine sound again. Where the hell was it coming from? Finn removed a glass from the cabinet above the sink and moved to the south kitchen wall. He placed the open end of the glass on the wall with his right ear pressing against the bottom of the glass. Methodically he slid the glass along the wall and listened for a potential source of the mysterious sounds. Finn repositioned the glass on the west wall and began a slow slide north. At the midpoint of the wall he abruptly stopped. The bells had rung again, louder than the last time. Finn's head shot up toward an air conditioning vent near the top of the wall. He grabbed a chair and as quickly as his knee would allow, he was standing on the chair, eye level with the metal vent. Finn's heart was beating excitedly. The sounds were definitely coming from the vent. The voices were starting again. Finn stood on his toes and pushed his right ear up to the vent. This time, he could hear the words.

Finn hopped to the kitchen floor, landing solely on his left leg. He put the kitchen chair back in place before returning to the living room sofa. He sat in the center of the sofa and took a deep, deliberate breath. Then he began to laugh. It began as a very shallow chuckle but quickly transitioned to a hearty belly laugh. Finn did everything he could to muffle his laughter. He certainly did not want to wake Candice.

At 6 AM Finn heard the sound of wheels rolling in the hallway. He sprung to the apartment door, hoping his intuition would be correct. It was. Pablo Rosales, the building superintendent, was rolling a maintenance cart down the floor toward the elevator.

"Excuse me."

"Yes?" Pablo looked apprehensively towards Finn.

"Can I ask you a question?" Finn interpreted Pablo's silence as an affirmative response, so he pressed on. "Do you know the lady who lives in 1602?"

"No." Pablo seemed uncomfortable. "She's an old lady who moved in a couple of months ago, but I haven't said a word to her. Why do you ask? And who are you?"

"I'm a friend of the family." Finn quickly answered Pablo's question and continued with his own queries. "Let me ask you something. Where is the nearest subway station?

"The 67the Avenue station is right downstairs."

"How close is the station?"

"Real close." Pablo elaborated further, "As a matter of fact, the platform is directly under this building."

Finn smiled. "Let me ask you something else. Can you hear the subway up on these floors?"

"Sure," Pablo responded matter-of-factly. "Especially late at light."

Finn tilted his head slightly. "Why late at night?"

"When it's late at night, there's very little noise in the area, so the subway noises come through loud and clear. They make their way out of the subway and through the AC vents in the building. Sometimes, people on the upper floors will be woken up by the tones from the train doors, and they can hear the conductor announcing over the train's public-address system that this stop is 67th Avenue."

Finn's smile grew broader as he extended his hand. "Thank you, my friend."

"Don't mention it, amigo." Pablo released the handshake still wondering what had just happened.

Finn yawned as he adjusted his butt in his chair. Several weeks had not caused his posterior to get used to the uncomfortable seat. He had caught a few hours of sleep before returning to the office to complete his reports on the Candice Rothchild case. Finn had tried to explain that she was only hearing the late-night sounds of the subway trains running below her building, but Candice was having none of that explanation. Candice seemed to like Finn, and obviously liked having him around, maybe because she had no other visitors during a normal day. Candice wanted Finn to continue his investigation, stating that money was no object. That statement would prompt a cash register sounding "ca-ching" from most other investigators, but Finn just couldn't fleece this misguided old woman. While in the apartment, Finn learned that Candice's only relative was a son who lived in Virginia. Ben Rothchild was a lawyer in the Richmond area, with two daughters in Virginia Tech. Under the pretext of asking her son if he had ever heard the sounds while he was in the process of renting the apartment for his mother, Finn was able to obtain Ben Rothchild's phone number.

"So, you see, Mr. Rothchild, I'm not going to take any money from your mom just because the subway sounds come into her building late at night."

Ben Rothchild was genuinely grateful. "I'll deal with my mother, but I must tell you Mr. Delaney, it's really refreshing to deal with someone who works ethically. You could have legally milked a load of money out of my mother, but you didn't. I won't forget this."

THE BEGINNING

OCTOBER 2nd – Finn paged through his contracts for August and September. He didn't realize he had dealt with so many crazy clients already. These contracts should have been filed but obviously, this duty had slipped his ace secretary's mind. Finn shook his head and chuckled. "File these please, Gladys." He dropped the contracts back on his desk, his private act making its point. It was 10 AM and Gladys was late again.

Finn heard the telltale sounds from the stairs. Eureka, his secretary would arrive in the office in ten minutes. Finn didn't feel like dealing with Gladys this morning. He wrote "Please File" on a yellow sticky note and stuck it on the top contract in the pile. He dropped the contracts in the middle of Gladys's desk and headed for the stairs. Gladys was taking a rest four steps from the top as Finn passed by.

"I'll be across the street," Finn mentioned without stopping.

"What else is new." Gladys responded.

Finn hesitated briefly, shook his head and continued out the door.

When the heavy oak door opened to his push, Finn's spirits rose. He was longing for a cup of Kevin's coffee.

"Look who's here – my regular first customer of the day." Kevin held a coffee cup up in his hand. "See, I was expecting you."

The cup had barely touched the bar when Finn's hands were on it and he was savoring his first sip. Finn took a deep, satisfied breath and placed the cup on the bar. "Just when I thought the Lord completely passed you by in the talent department – you produce this."

"Screw you Finbar." Kevin made a fake grab for Finn's cup. "I should take that back."

"Never!" Finn chuckled as he protected the cup with his arms. "By the way, why did you have the coffee ready for me today? What's the occasion?"

"I know my social graces." Kevin stated. "And I know how to show gratitude."

"What?"

"This coffee at the ready is my way of saying thanks for putting in a good word for me with Tommy Clancy."

Finn slapped the bar. "You got the job?"

Kevin nodded. "I start tonight. Four nights a week from 6 to 10."

"Good luck!" Finn raised his coffee cup.

"You sure you don't want a little pick me up in that coffee." Kevin displayed the bottle of Bailey's.

"No thanks." Finn said. "And you shouldn't have it either – you're working tonight."

"Great advice," Kevin commented as he poured a double shot into his coffee.

"Hey!" Finn pointed his finger at Kevin. "Don't screw this up. I went out on a limb for you with Tommy."

"I know I know. I got this covered. Here - increase your knowledge." Kevin slid the New York Post to Finn while retaining the Daily News for himself. Kevin wet his index finger on his tongue and turned the page. "OK, let's see how long it takes to depress me today. Kevin made only one page turn before stretching his arms out to the side

"Look at this. This poor young girl killed and thrown in a dumpster. It's a damn shame."

Kevin was referring to the murder of a 21-year old female who was found in a dumpster behind a lower Manhattan housing project.

Finn continued with his own paper. “What are you gonna do, Kev. There’s always gonna be sickos in the world.

OCTOBER 22nd - Finn yawned as he trudged up the steps. Why was he feeling so guilty at being a little bit late to the office? Gladys was late almost every day. Besides, he was the boss, wasn't he? Couldn't the boss sleep in once in a while? He emerged from the stairs to face an empty office. Finn shook his head and sighed. Apparently, Gladys had not come to work this morning. As Finn walked around his desk he realized his assessment had been premature. A yellow sticky note was resting in the middle of Finn's desk blotter. He snatched the note and brought it close to his face in order to make out her incredibly small handwriting

"Went to doctor's appointment – be back later – call (804) 878-4576"

A second cryptic message seemed to read:

T.C. here – not happy – come back

Finn had no idea what the second message meant, so he turned his attention to the phone number. He flipped the note back on his desk and frowned. Nice old lady or not, the situation wasn't working out. This was at least the third time Gladys had left a phone number on a note without any reference as to whose number it was. Finn realized he was going to have to talk to his dad sooner or later regarding Gladys.

Finn grimaced as he settled into his favorite chair and held onto the expression as he began to dial. He hated calling a number when he had no idea who he was calling. Finn received a temporary reprieve from making the call when the sound of footsteps began resonating from the stairwell. The mystery of the second message was solved by the appearance of Tommy Clancy.

No additional clues were required. Finn knew exactly why Tommy was paying him a visit. It had been a little more than three weeks since he had held his nose and told Tommy how much Kevin had changed, and how he really should give him another chance. Kevin had begun working nights at Simon's three weeks earlier, and Tommy's appearance indicated that Kevin had likely screwed up yet another opportunity.

Tommy slowly crossed the office with arms outstretched.

"What the fuck, Finn! What the fuck!"

Finn fought back a smile and tried to sound concerned,

"What's wrong Tommy?"

"You know what's wrong. You vouched for that clown, and I was stupid enough to believe you."

Finn pointed to the comfortable chair. "Relax, Tommy. Sit down and tell me what you're talking about."

Tommy eased into the ergonomic chair. "I'm talking about that lying, no good, moron friend of yours."

"He's your friend too, Tommy." Finn corrected.

"Not anymore!" Tommy shot back

"What happened?"

"He fooled me," Tommy said. "After three weeks I was beginning to believe that he really may have changed. Everything was working out great."

"So, what happened," Finn questioned.

"Reality!" Tommy exclaimed. "It's just not in his nature to be responsible. Two nights ago, he was scheduled to work alone until closing. Normally, I have at least two or three detectives working, but I was short-handed, so Kevin was my only coverage. In other words, Finbar, it was really important for your friend to come to work."

"I guess he called in sick or something." Finn stated.

"He didn't call in or anything. He just didn't show up. So last night, after 24-hours among the missing, this guy shows up for work like there's nothing wrong. I ask him what happened, and he says he's sorry, but that he spent the last day in the hospital with his father."

"What happened to his dad?" Finn liked Mr. Malone and had legitimately become concerned by the story.

"He told me that his old man cut his fingers off in the printing press."

It took all of Finn's self-control to keep from bursting out in laughter. Both Finn and Tommy knew that Kevin's dad worked on the printing presses at the New York Daily News.

Tommy continued, "He tells me that he's so distraught, he loses all track of time. So, I very calmly tell him to get me documentation from the hospital. Now, he gets this look on his face like he never considered having to document his bullshit story. He very weakly tells me he'll get the documentation before leaving my office."

"Did he bring the documentation?"

"Really, Finn?" Tommy raised his eyebrows. "About a half hour later he comes back to my office and says he has to talk to me. He's looking from side to side and begins talking all secretive. This guy had the nerve to tell me that the hospital would not have a record of his father's presence because his father actually works for the CIA."

"That was it?" Finn asked.

"Yup!" Tommy continued. "I didn't say a word. I just went back to my paperwork and he eventually left my office and never came back. At least I'll give him credit for understanding when his goose is cooked."

"I'm really sorry, Tommy!" Finn tried to appear contrite, but he couldn't stop the grin from appearing, and then quickly transitioned to a full-fledged laugh. Similarly, Tommy's sneer made the same brief journey to laughter.

"Your friend is one incredible asshole," Tommy laughed. "CIA? Gimme a friggin break!"

Finn required a good fifteen minutes after Tommy's departure to regain his composure. It was now time to try the mystery phone number.

"Hello."

"Hello – This is Finn Delaney returning your call."

"Thanks for returning my call so promptly, Mr. Delaney. It's nice to talk to you again."

There was definitely a familiar quality to this pleasant sounding male voice, but Finn couldn't identify it.

"Yeah, it's great to talk to you again too." Finn was biding his time until something in the conversation could trigger recognition.

"My mother said to say hello to you. She really thinks the world of you."

Finn's brain was on overdrive. Wait a minute – Virginia phone number – mother who likes me. He was ready to take his shot.

"Mr. Rothchild?"

Ben Rothchild seemed momentarily confused. “Um, who did you think you were talking to?”

“I’m sorry Mr. Rothchild. I still need that first cup of coffee for the day.” Finn supposed that was a good recovery line despite the fact that he already had a Dunkin Donuts caffeine fix.

“That’s OK, Finn.” Ben Rothchild chuckled and became more familiar. “I’m hoping you can help an old friend of my wife.”

“I’ll try.” Finn’s eyes darted back and forth on his desktop before settling on a legal notepad. He snatched the pad and grabbed a pen from his top drawer. “Go ahead, Mr. Rothchild.”

“Ben, please.” Ben Rothchild corrected before continuing with the details. “Susan Garland was best friends with my wife and she still lives in Queens. Susan has been a widow for the past twelve years and she has one child – a 21-year old daughter named Chelsea.”

“Where does Chelsea live?” Finn kept scribbling on the legal pad.

“She lives at home with her mother, but that’s the reason I’m calling you.”

Finn stopping writing. “I don’t think I’m following you Mr. Ro….Ben.”

Ben Rothchild clarified the situation. “She missing.”

“Missing?” Finn repeated

“Yes, she hasn’t been heard from in two weeks and Susan’s going out of her mind.”

“Isn’t this a police matter?” Finn asked

"I thought so," Ben responded, "But the police told her that Chelsea is not a missing person – something about her being 21 years old."

Finn was having trouble visualizing a role for him. "I don't know Ben. I don't really think there's anything I can…."

Ben Rothchild wouldn't let Finn complete his statement. "Please Finn. Just call Susan. You'd be doing me a big favor."

Finn picked up the pen again. "Sure Ben. Let me have her information."
Finn remained in dialing mode. He wanted to get this over with.

"Susan Garland, please."

"Who is calling?"

With only three words, Finn already had a profile of the woman on the other end of the phone – emotionless. If he didn't know any better, he might have been communicating with an automated robotic voice, except that most of the automated voices are programmed to sound upbeat and pleasant.

"This is Finn Delaney, ma'am."

"What's this about?"

The response took Finn by surprise. He just assumed Ben Rothchild had thoroughly briefed this lady, and that she would be waiting for his call with bated breath.

"I'm a private investigator. Ben Rothchild told me…." The woman cut him off.

"Yes, Christine told me you might be calling," she acknowledged, her voice still devoid of emotion.

"I'd like to come by and talk to you when you're available."

"I'm available Sunday morning at 11:00 – 42-28 12th Street in Broad Channel."

Finn babbled on for approximately twenty seconds before he realized that Susan Garland was not on the line. "Oh, well," he verbalized to himself while accessing the calendar on his iPhone. "I guess Sunday at 11 is OK."

Finn's caseload was currently empty, but he did have a lot of reports to prepare from his most recent activities with his cheaters and crazies. It was 2:00 PM on a Friday afternoon when Finn glanced across the office. These reports were the job of his secretary, weren't they? He bit his lip as he watched Gladys crocheting at her desk. Elderly or not, it was time for Finn to put his foot down and take control of the office.

"Gladys!" Finn called with his best boss voice.

"Yes, Finn." Gladys peered over at Finn above her reading glasses.

What he wanted to say was "Get to work!" but what came out was "Why don't you go home early. I got things covered."

Thirty minutes later Finn sat in the office alone, working on his reports. He found it hard to focus on his work because he was disgusted with his inability to actually ask Gladys to work. Finn became more bitter with each peck on the keyboard. His dad thrust this old lady upon him, so he would insist that his dad remove her. It was 6:00 PM when Finn closed the laptop. Enough obsessing on Gladys. It was time to go across the street and obsess on something else.

Entering the Shamrock after 6 PM on a Friday night could be dangerous. He wasn't sure what time the hostess began work, so there was a chance he could walk right into Meghan. This was a chance he was willing to take, however, because he wanted to deal with Kevin while still appropriately outraged. It mattered little that Kevin got relieved at 5 PM, as there was one hundred percent certainty that he would be sitting at the bar drinking at 6 PM.

Finn experienced an immediate sense of relief when he pushed open the heavy oak door. The hostess podium was empty. Perhaps the hostess didn't go on duty until 7 PM. He scanned the bar and confirmed that death and taxes were not the only two thing you could count on. You could also count on finding Kevin Malone sitting at the bar whenever he was not working.

Finn tried to conjure up just the right words to express his disappointment, outrage, and shock at Kevin's blatant disregard for his endorsement. His thought process was completely cut off by the sound of a female voice.

"Hi, Finn." Finn spun around to see Meghan advancing from the dining room. Obviously, she had been seating some early dinner guests when he entered the pub.

"Hey, Meg. How are you?"

"I'm great, how about you"

Finn feared he had entered into this vortex of endless greetings that he would be unable to break free of. He tried to extricate himself with something Meghan would understand.

"I have to go see Kevin. He's been acting like a real jerk."

Meg rolled her eyes. “Some things never change. What did he do now?”

Finn had Meghan howling with delight at the tale of Tommy Clancy, a job, a rouge printing press and the Central Intelligence Agency.”

“Oh my God!” Meg wiped her eyes. “He is too much!”

“Yes, he is.” Finn responded. He also made an amazing discovery. Finn had enjoyed this brief, light conversation with Meg. But now, it was on to Kevin.

“Great talking to you, Finn.”

Finn thought for a moment before responding. “Yeah, it was nice, wasn’t it?”

“We should do it more often,” Meg exclaimed.

“We should.” That was as far as Finn could bring himself to go as he turned and headed toward the end of the bar.

Kevin was always on the prowl for gossip, and he had seen the conversation between Finn and Meg. “What’s this I just saw, you dirty dog. You’re finally going to trap Meg in your web, aren’t you?

Finn did his best to ignore the comment. He needed to keep the momentum of his outrage fresh.

“Never mind Meg, you jerk. I must have been out of my mind to give you a recommendation.”

Kevin sported the look of a wounded puppy. “What are you talking about?”

Finn kept up his intensity. “Let me refresh your memory. How are your father’s fingers?”

“Oh, that,” Kevin chuckled.

"Yeah, that – you moron. My credibility with Clancy is completely shot now."

Kevin attempted to switch to an indignant strategy. "Hey, wait a minute. What if my dad really did cut his fingers off? You'd feel pretty bad now, wouldn't you?

Finn's voice rose a level. "But he didn't cut his fingers off, did he?"

"Yeah, but he could have!" Kevin fired back defiantly.

Finn paused for a moment and squinted. "What the hell does that even mean?"

Kevin switched to a friendly tone. "Why don't you just forget about it. That job wasn't for me anyway." He waved to the bartender. "Hey Jimmy! Give Finn a beer. It will calm him down."

Finn slid off the stool. "I don't want your beer. I'm out of here!"

Finn took two steps before Kevin called to him, a wry smile on his face. "You have to admit it was a good story."

Finn could hold in his laughter no longer. "You are an asshole," he snickered as he backed toward the exit.

"And what's going on with you and our little hostess?"

"You're a tremendous asshole!" Finn grinned as he passed through the door.

OCTOBER 25th - Finn hesitated at the driver's door, eyeing the sky nervously. The clouds that had been wispy and white earlier in the morning were now darker and more dense. As he drove from the curb he could sense a coming downpour. Finn turned south on Woodhaven Blvd. and immediately let loose with a string of profanities. He assumed the traffic would be light on a late Sunday morning.

The heavy traffic provided Finn with time for reflection. For reasons unknown, he suddenly experienced something of an epiphany. Finn had driven on this stretch of Cross Bay Blvd. countless times on the way to Rockaway Beach, first with his parents, and in more recent times with his friends. The vision of tooling down the boulevard with Kevin and Meg was fixed in his brain, especially the image of Meghan. Until this moment, however, he had never really thought about the area he was passing through.

For many New Yorkers like Finn, Broad Channel was a blur of a neighborhood on the way to the beach. In reality, the community was a quirky neighborhood, maybe the most unusual in all of Queens or even New York City. It was out in the middle of Jamaica Bay, surrounded by water on all sides, connected to the rest of Queens by two bridges and one subway. The narrow, mile-long neighborhood was populated by several thousand residents, many of them active or retired firefighters, police officers and other civil servants, such as school teacher Susan Garland. Some families had been there for generations. Broad Channel was a unique little slice of New York City - an island tethered to Queens by bridges with squadrons of Brandt geese touching down on one side of the neighborhood, planes lifting off at Kennedy Airport at the other side, and Midtown Manhattan an hour and a world away.

Finn easily found a parking space on Cross Bay Blvd. and 12th Street. The anticipated rainstorm had not materialized, but the sky was still ominous. There was very little commercial activity on the boulevard, which Finn found a bit odd. Whereas just about all of Cross Bay Blvd. north and south of Broad Channel was lined with stores and commercial enterprises of every size and shape, much of this stretch of the road was lined with private homes, many of them newly aluminum sided as a constant reminder of the devastation Superstorm Sandy inflicted on the community several years earlier.

As Finn stood on Cross Bay Blvd. he felt he could almost touch water on both sides. He walked along 12th street watching egrets pick their way meticulously through the mud flats, acting as if they owned the place. The birds served as such a distraction that Finn was forced to perform an about face when he realized he had bypassed his address.

Finn turned and took in the entirety of the front yard while waiting for a response to the doorbell. It wasn't much of a yard. In fact, this concrete slab surrounded by a 4-foot chain link fence was 20-feet x 5-feet at the most. Finn scanned up and down the block and realized this front yard was not unique. Most of the very small bungalow homes within his view sported similar tiny front yards.

The moment the door opened, Finn immediately knew the one word to best describe Susan Garland – tired. The pleasant features of this attractive middle age lady were masked by red eyes surrounded by lines and bags, make-up slightly smeared, and blond hair pulled up rather messily into a pony tail.

"Come in, please."

The dimly lit living room seemed too large for this tiny bungalow. Finn stopped in the center of the room but responded to Susan's sweeping motion of her right arm, guiding Finn to the dominating feature of the room. The huge mahogany table took up most of the space the dark room had to offer. Left without a table cloth, it appeared to Finn that the table stood defiantly, daring guests to ruin the perfectly varnished shine with unworthy fingerprints. Finn settled into an ornate-looking chair almost as uncomfortable as the one at his desk. It was clear to him that this dining table in a home without a dining room was meant to be the showpiece of the home. Two tall, silver candelabras commanded attention from the center of the table, holding smooth white candles whose wax probably never dripped.

Finn noticed no television or bookshelf, and the only other attraction drawing his attention dominated the cream-colored wall he was facing. An array of photographs hung the entire length of the upper half of the wall. The photos were black and white, not casual family snaps, but arranged in a most professional display. Finn knew virtually nothing of art, yet he instinctively sensed he would likely find similar photo displays inside an art gallery.

The photos contained many people, but one recurring subject seemed to dominate. Proceeding from left to right, the pictures seemed to document the history of a pretty young girl from toddler to young adulthood.

"Would you like coffee, sir?"

"No thank you, Mrs. Garland. And please, call me Finn."

A weak smile appeared on Susan's face. "And you please call me Susan."

Susan sat at the table opposite Finn, and for a brief moment both parties studied each other, trying to determine who should speak first. Finn decided to break the ice.

"Is that your daughter?" Finn nodded toward the photo display.

Susan turned in her chair, eying the wall. "Yes, that's my Chelsea from about two years of age right up to…." Susan hesitated and stared into space. "I think the last photo is from about six months ago."

"She's very pretty." Finn would have made this observation under any circumstances, but in this case, he really meant his assessment. Finn studied several of Chelsea's recent photos. She had an understated beauty, maybe because she appeared to be so disarmingly unaware of her prettiness. Finn was accustomed to a bombardment of female photos on Facebook that screamed "Look at me – I'm the fairest of them all!" Chelsea's photos were different. She wasn't beautiful in the classical sense; no flowing golden curls or ivory skin; no piercing eyes of green. In the pictures she seemed shorter than average and certainly larger than a catwalk model, but in her ordinariness, she was stunning. Something radiated from within that rendered her irresistible.

Finn took a legal pad out of his bag and gingerly placed it on the highly polished table. "I guess you should tell me what happened?" Finn instantly realized this what not the opening line of a hard-boiled gumshoe that would instill confidence in his client – but what the hell, he had to begin somewhere, didn't he?

It really wasn't much of a story. Three weeks earlier Susan had received a phone call from Chelsea informing her that she was going out after work in Manhattan. That call was the last time Susan heard from her daughter.

Finn realized he had a load of background information to obtain, and he scribbled furiously as Susan responded to his queries.

Name: Chelsea Marie Garland

Age: 21-years 10-months

Height: 5' 5"

Weight: 130 pounds

Hair: Blond

Eyes: Green

Education: BS Accounting – Queens College

Occupation: Recently started job as Junior Accountant for Meyers, Werth, and Sloan, a mid-size Manhattan accounting firm.

Boyfriend: None

Finn was not surprised that Susan characterized her daughter as being a very good girl. "I never had a single problem with her, even during the tough teenage years after her father passed away."

Finn was uncomfortable, but continued probing. "How did your husband die?"

"Lung cancer. He was a fireman. I'm still fighting with the God damn city to make his death 9/11 related."

A meek "I'm sorry," was Finn's weak response.

Susan shrugged. "All that doesn't really matter now, does it?"

Finn's responses became weaker and all he could manage was a silent shrug to Susan's statements.

Susan continued without a question. "Such a bright girl, and not just book smart. Chelsea is loaded with common sense – I guess you would call her street smart."

"What did you do when Chelsea didn't come home?" Finn momentarily put the pen down and flexed his right hand.

"When I couldn't get her on her phone, I called a couple of her neighborhood friends, but they weren't with her that night and didn't know where she was going."

"Work friends?"

"I don't know of any work friends. She only worked in Manhattan for a couple of months."

Finn resumed his note taking. "Then what did you do?"

"I called the police and told them all of what I told you."

"What did the police tell you?"

"Not much. The two young uniformed officers – a man and a woman – took a lot of notes like you and said they would prepare a report."

"Anything else with the police?" Finn continued.

"The next day a detective came to see me. He told me that they would do what they could, but that without any evidence of foul play, someone who was almost 22-years old was an adult and not a missing person."

"What was the detective's name?"

Susan left the room for no more than five seconds before returning with a business card extended in her right hand. Finn accepted the card with a nod.

DETECTIVE ALEX DELVECCHIO INTELLIGENCE DIVISION.

Intelligence Division? That was odd, wasn't it? His extremely limited NYPD experience prevented Finn from definitively answering his own question. "Anything else, Susan?"

Susan took a deep, deliberate breath and produced a folded piece of paper, presumably from her pocket. She slid the paper across the table into Finn's waiting hand. Throughout the interview Finn sensed Susan's self-conscious nature in her attempts to stifle her tears when the conversation turned emotional. Now, however, as Finn unfolded the paper, she finally gave way to the enormity of her grief. She sobbed into her hands and the tears dripped between her fingers, raining down on the highly shined table. Her breathing was ragged, gasping, as the remaining strength vacated her body. Finn became increasingly uncomfortable as Susan's head sank until her forehead contacted the table, her fingers raking the tabletop and leaving scratch marks on the room's showpiece. Finn wasn't sure of the right thing to do. Should he walk around the table and hug her, or should he try to find some words of consolation. He did neither and instead read the handwritten contents of the freshly unfolded paper.

Dear Mom,

I know this is hard for you, but I have decided to leave and start a completely new life. I met a great guy online and I have gone to live with him on the west coast. I know this is hard for you – it is also hard for me, but I have to do it this

way. Please don't try to find me. Once I am settled I will contact you. Please be patient with me and always remember that I love you.
Chelsea.

Finn glanced up and was relieved to see that a degree of composure had returned to Susan. As a matter of fact, grief had transitioned to anger as she pointed at the letter.

"That," she sneered, "arrived two days after the detective was here. It's preposterous! We were a team. She would never do this. Would a smart girl leave without taking anything?" Her voice took on a tone of exasperation. "It's not even her handwriting."

Finn tapped his pen lightly on the legal pad. "Did anything else happen?"

"The day after the letter came, the same detective came back and asked if I had heard anything from Chelsea. I showed him the letter and he said it confirmed that she had left on her own volition and was not missing. He told me to be patient and that eventually he was sure Chelsea would reach out to me. He also made a point of telling me to call him immediately if Chelsea contacted me."

The silence in the room was deafening. Finn put his pen down and lightly tapped his fingers on the pad. He had no idea what to tell Susan. Susan Garland, on the other hand, knew exactly what she wanted to say.

"Please help me." She began. "I have no one to help. No family – no local friends – the police won't help." Susan reached across the table and took hold of Finn's hands. Finn had never seen a more desperate look in anyone's eyes. "Please, help me find my little girl."

Finn gently squeezed Susan's hands and allowed a slight smile to emerge.

"Of course, I'll help you, Susan." At that moment, Finbar Delaney, private investigator, had no idea how he was going to help.

Finn adjusted the headset properly around his right ear. Communications were critical or lives could be needlessly lost. He tested the coms with the others – everything was functioning properly. Finn reviewed the tactical plan for the evening – an offensive surge. He realized casualties would be high, but that was the cost of war. It may have looked like his room, but Finn was the leading force in a command and control center. The offensive was about to begin and his forces were the tip of the spear. A Sunday night "Call of Duty" marathon was about to begin.

A few years ago, Finn's parents believed he would outgrow video games. Instead, Finn outgrew the shame associated with being a 25-year-old who still liked to sit in his room gaming. Finn loved video games and he was tired of apologizing for his hobby.

The artillery, automatic gunfire, and general carnage did not prevent Finn from hearing his father enter the house downstairs. Finn wanted to confer with his dad regarding the Chelsea Garland case, and he knew he had a very limited window of opportunity. Once Sunday Night Football began, Patrick Delaney was glued to the television. A conference would be impossible during the game and Finn knew it. A temporary armistice was declared.

"What's up Fineous?" Patrick inquired while reaching for a beer in the refrigerator.

"I wanted to talk to you about this new case I have – a missing girl."

"How old is she?" Patrick strained to see if there were any chips hidden in the back of a cabinet.

"Almost twenty-two."

Patrick started drifting into the living room. "Not much of a missing person. More like an adult who wanted to get out of her house."

"I know," Finn responded. "But I told this mother I would help her. Isn't there anything I can do for her?"

Patrick settled into his easy chair. "OK, tell me what you got."

Finn finished the briefing. Patrick sat back in the easy chair, thoughtfully stroking his chin. "Well, I have to admit you have some interesting facts here. You have a goodbye letter from the daughter, but she didn't take one personal belonging with her. And why is the detective from the Intelligence Division on this? It doesn't make sense."

"That's what I thought," Finn concurred. "But what should I do?"

"The girl and her mother live in Broad Channel, right?" Patrick asked.

"Correct."

"That's in the 100th Precinct. You need to talk to the detectives there – see what they have on this. Donny McHugh is an old buddy of mine. He's in the 100th Squad. I'll call him for you."

"Thanks, dad."

"And now, Fineous, if you don't mind it's time for the kickoff."

Finn didn't mind. He still had a bloody battle to win upstairs.

HALLOWEEN, NYPD STYLE

OCTOBER 29th - The light drizzle did not necessitate the use of an umbrella for the two-block walk from his parking space to the precinct. Finn paused at the bottom of the three steps. During his all too brief NYPD career he had never been to the 100th Precinct. This ancient-looking three-story flagstone and brick structure on the Rockaway Peninsula did not seem representative of the citizen friendly NYPD mantra that had been drilled into his head during academy training. There was no flicker of light visible behind the thick wooden doors and the surrounding green lamps did not radiate a welcoming atmosphere.

In pushing through the doors, Finn entered an interior world that seemed to be the perfect complement to the old, unwelcoming exterior. He could hear the radiators thrumming at the base of the wall behind the reception desk, filling the air with the sound of pressure released and pressure renewed. Officers in blue-black coats and bulletproof vests came and went, slicking the worn terrazzo floor with rainy footprints. Except for the jittery hissing, it seemed quiet inside the station house.

Finn stood obediently behind the low gate forbidding civilians from entering the sacred ground of police officers.

"May I help you?"

Finn followed the voice to his left, and his jaw dropped. Approaching the gate was a tall stocky male wearing an official NYPD cap and tie with his police officer shield pinned conspicuously on his left breast – perfectly appropriate attire for one of New York City's Finest. Triggering Finn's astonishment was the bright orange animal print tunic. It took a moment for the light bulb to illuminate above Finn's head. This cop was dressed like Fred Flintstone. But wait a minute. Fred Flintstone wasn't the only insanity present in the house. Behind the large oak desk sat the precinct desk sergeant, intently writing entries in the precinct blotter. Nothing odd here, except that the desk officer wore a metallic suit like the hero in the movie Robocop. This Robocop suit even had the NYPD logo printed on his chest, ala Superman.

"May I help you?" Fred Flintstone repeated his question, this time with a slight tone of annoyance.

Finn turned his attention back toward Fred. "I have an appointment to see Detective McHugh."

Officer Flintstone swung open the gate. "PDU is on the second floor to the right."

As Finn crossed the creaking wood floor Robocop never looked up from his blotter. As he began ascending the stairs he felt satisfied at not having to ask what PDU meant. Even with his limited experience he knew those letters were the abbreviation for Precinct Detective Unit.

The door was open, and Finn could see only one person visible inside the office. Finn cleared his throat and stood in the doorway. "Detective McHugh?"

The lone office occupant closed his newspaper. "Delaney?"

Finn nodded, still planted at the doorway.

"Well come on in lad and have a seat."

Finn instantly assessed Don McHugh as one of those terminally upbeat guys who never seemed to be in a bad mood. He also theorized that when a dark mood did befall him, Detective McHugh could probably break a man in half with his bare hands. Even in a seated position he appeared massive in both height and width. McHugh pulled on the red tie that hung loosely around his white dress shirt with an open top button.

"How is the Chief? I haven't seen him in ages. I was shocked as shit to hear from him the other day."

"He's good," Finn responded.

"Yeah, he was telling me what happened to you. What a shame no one could do anything for you."

Finn realized that in the old school world of NYPD politics, Don was not referring to the inability of doctors to repair his knee to acceptable standards. Rather, he felt it was a shame that no phone call could be made to someone with the juice to keep Finn on the job or to at least figure out a way to get a three quarters line of duty pension authorized.

Don McHugh stopped playing with his tie and rubbed his hands together. "So, Mr. Delaney private eye – what can I help you with?"

Finn took a deep breath in anticipation of his story but stopped abruptly. "Before I start, I just have to ask. What the heck is going on downstairs?"

Don McHugh leaned back in his chair and let out a laugh befitting a man of his stature. "They're getting ready for haunted precinct night."

Finn's blank expression prompted Don to continue. "It started last year – ordered directly from the Borough Commander. One night around Halloween we have to turn the precinct into some type of haunted, apocalyptic fright zone. Last year hundreds of people in the Rockaway community gathered outside of the precinct to take a walkthrough."

"Is it scary?" Finn inquired.

"I brought my grandson last year and it scared the shit out of him. I think he's still shaking. Some of the cops downstairs go overboard dressing like zombies, and jumping around like maniacs." Don shook his head as his mood seemed to sour. "Who would have ever thought we'd be doing stupid shit like this in the NYPD." The somber tone quickly turned back to upbeat. "At least there's gonna be a hell of a lot of candy around here for the next week."

Finn relayed the very short story of Chelsea Garland and then hoped he would receive something – anything that he could go back to Susan with that would let her know he was making an effort on her behalf.

"Hmm," Don McHugh stroked his chin. "I do recall the name, but not much else."

Don's huge figure rose from his seat and lumbered to an array of metal filing cabinets at the opposite end of the office. Finn found something totally appropriate with this action. What else should he expect from a grizzled old detective in an ancient police precinct? Did he really think Don McHugh was going to insert a flash drive into a USB port?

Don returned to his desk with a file folder. He began by telling Finn what he already knew. "Not really much here. The girl is almost twenty-two – not really a missing person, you know."

"I know," Finn said, "but the mother really thinks there's something more than meets the eye here."

"They all do," Don stated as he scanned the remaining documents in the file. "Here's something. At 11:35 PM on October 1st, the young lady withdrew a thousand dollars from a Bank of America ATM on First Avenue and 33rd Street in Manhattan. The five says the video in the bank showed she was alone and did not appear to be under duress. The video also shows her leave her iPhone at the ATM."

Finn was immediately pleased – not so much from the information, but from his recognition of more NYPD jargon. He knew that a "five" was slang for form DD5, which was simply an investigative report, prepared by a detective.

"That's it." Don shut the file folder. "Closed to patrol."

Finn's string of jargon recognition had run out. "Closed to patrol?"

"Yeah, technically, it's an open case, but, nothing is going to happen unless a patrol cop stumbles on her."

"What about the letter?"

Don re-opened the file. "What letter? There's no letter in here?"

"The letter where Chelsea tells her mother she's leaving home. The detective from the Intelligence Division knows about it."

Now Detective McHugh wore a similar expression to Finn's first glance at Fred Flintstone. "Why would Intel. Be involved with this?"

"I don't know, but the mother told me Detective Delvecchio from Intelligence has contacted her several times."

Don McHugh completely altered Finn's archaic perception of him when he settled in behind a different desk and activated the power on the desktop computer.

Don stroked the keyboard for several minutes before leaning back and again stroking his chin. "There is a Detective Alex Delvecchio in Intel." He shrugged as he continued. "But for the life of me I have no idea why Intel. would be involved in this."

Finn thanked Detective McHugh and began to make his exit.

"Wait up." McHugh called. "I'll walk you out. Besides, I want to grab a handful of candy."

There were now more costumed ghouls and super heroes roaming around the first floor of the precinct. Finn and McHugh walked past the precinct desk but were stopped in their tracks by a creepy voice.

"Good Evening." The voice sounded exactly like every old Bela Lugosi Dracula movie Finn had ever seen. He turned to the direction of the voice and was not surprised to see a very authentic-looking Count Dracula peeking out from behind a cape.

"Stick around. I may want to put the bite on you later." The Count laughed maniacally as he drifted across the floor. Finn and McHugh continued to the precinct door.

Finn extended his hand and chuckled, "It gets crazier and crazier around here tonight, doesn't it?"

Detective McHugh accepted the handshake. "You don't know the half of it. Count Dracula back there – that was Deputy Inspector Collins, the precinct commanding officer."

Finn's eyes widened, and his mouth dropped open as McHugh released the handshake. "Let me tell you something, kid. That knee injury of yours may well have been a blessing."

THE HOMELESS LADY

NOVEMBER 2nd - Finn was dreading his return to Cross Bay Blvd. That helpless, hopeless look from Susan Garland as she sat across the table during their last encounter was emblazoned in his memory. He was aware that the longer Chelsea remained missing, the better the odds for an unhappy ending, and it was bound to get progressively more depressing meeting with Susan as the last fragments of hope trickled away.

"Suck it up Delaney," Finn mouthed in a personal pep talk as he stepped out of his car. Aside from the passing light traffic, it was quiet on Cross Bay during this late morning weekday. When Finn called Susan, he thought he would have to come see her in the late afternoon when she finished teaching her second graders, but the time of the visit turned out to be irrelevant. Susan had become such a wreck that she could no longer teach. She had to take an indefinite leave of absence.

Finn began to compose his thoughts as he walked on Cross Bay toward 12th Street. The rattle of a supermarket cart shook him from his concentration. With no stores nearby, that sound was not a normal part of the street's auditory makeup. An old cart, rusted and full of tin cans shook as it passed over the uneven sidewalk slabs, a woman of unknown age behind it. Finn stared for a moment before he caught himself. With the homeless, it was hard to get a bearing on their age. The woman was dressed in untold layers of fragmenting wool, completely inappropriate for the mild, early November midday. Her hair was tied back, but still clumped with grease, and as she shuffled along, her head moved back and forth, unsteady like there was a personal earthquake beneath her inadequate shoes.

Finn gulped when the sound of the cart stopped. He was going to have to walk right past the woman who was now sitting on the curb on the south corner of 12th Street. Finn feared he had not ended his stare soon enough evidenced by the glare he was getting in return. As he turned on 12th Street he looked away. It certainly wasn't a friendly look he was receiving. As Finn waited at Susan's front door, he could still see the homeless woman perched on the curb. The distance made him uncertain, but it did appear that she was still staring at him. The homeless were an unfortunate fact of life in New York City, but Finn found it very odd to find a homeless person trudging along the street in a middle class residential neighborhood in Queens.

As the meeting with Susan began, Finn's trepidation transitioned into reality. As uncomfortable as he had been in the presence of Susan's emotional roller coaster ride during his initial meeting, her present state was more disturbing. Susan sat in the same position across the large mahogany table, but this time she was completely devoid of emotions. Finn was tempted to inquire if she was on any medications, but he realized such a question would be totally inappropriate. Her blank stare was catatonic-like and never changed throughout their information exchange. Finn was very troubled by Susan's condition. He had no psychological training, but it did not take a psychiatrist to recognize that there were not many levels of depression lower than Susan's present depth.

There was no visible reaction to Finn's information regarding the ATM withdrawal. Susan spoke with a zombie-like monotone in informing Finn that Detective Delvecchio had called every day asking if she had heard from Chelsea. She further stated that Delvecchio had made an unannounced visit yesterday to again ask if Chelsea had contacted her. Finn hadn't noticed earlier, but Susan had apparently been holding a business card during their conversation. When she mentioned Delvecchio's visit she held up the card in her right hand. Finn noticed that it was just one of Delvecchio's NYPD business cards, but there was something different about it.

"Excuse me Susan, could I please see that card?"

The table was wide enough that she had to slide it across the highly shined surface. Finn's attention went directly to the black ink writing on the back of the card.

DETECTIVE STANISLAS KARPINSKI

Finn held up the card, with the rear side writing facing Susan. "Who's this?"

"Oh, there was another detective with Delvecchio. He didn't have a card, so he wrote his name on the back of Delvecchio's card."

"Was this guy from the Intelligence Division too?"

Finn sensed that his question annoyed Susan to the maximum level her emotionless condition would allow. "I don't know where he was from. He didn't say much. It was just like the phone calls. They just wanted to make sure that I called them immediately if I hear from Chelsea."

Finn wanted to wish Susan good luck and tell her there was nothing more he could do, but before the door closed behind him, he said he would keep working and would get back to her in a few days.

As Finn walked east on 12th street his body suddenly sprung to alert. He had forgotten all about her. The homeless lady and her shopping cart were still on Cross Bay. Finn decided to employ a tactic he was taught in the police academy. A social science instructor had told the class that EDPs (emotionally disturbed persons) seem to sense fear and apprehension in a person, so the worst thing you can do if an EDP is staring at you is to look away. As Finn drew closer to the corner, icy stare was met with icy stare. When he turned right to continue walking on Cross Bay towards his parked car, he turned his head to the left to keep his eyes locked on the homeless lady. The stare down made him realize that this woman was probably much younger than he had originally perceived. When he turned away as he approached his car, Finn was sure he heard the woman growling and hissing at him. When he started the engine, he hesitated before shifting into drive. Finn smiled as he realized that his police academy training had finally been of some use.

The next morning Finn was back in his usual morning habitat, and the coffee smelled especially fresh. Finn had come to the realization years ago that no matter what crazy hijinks Kevin was involved with, he always forgave him and moved forward. Finn understood the nature of their relationship when he explained on more than one occasion that Kevin was like dog crap on his shoe – infuriating and almost impossible to totally get rid of.

Kevin took a break from his Irish Coffee to flip through the New York Post.

"Hey, look," Kevin exclaimed. "They caught the mope that killed that hot young girl."

"What are you talking about?" Finn momentarily interrupted his appreciation of the coffee.

"You mean you don't know," Kevin responded sarcastically. "I thought you were on top of all the world news."

Finn grabbed the edge of the paper and slid it along the bar until it was in front of him. The photo on the front page instantly jogged his memory. Pretty, twenty-one-year-old Cynthia Dubois smiled at him from under the bold headline – KILLER CAUGHT. Several weeks earlier this unfortunate young beauty had been found dead in a lower Manhattan dumpster, and the city could now rest a little easier with the murderer in custody. Finn studied the photo adjacent to Cynthia. Three stone-faced detectives led a handcuffed Bobby Lee Curtis out of the 7th Precinct station house. Finn shook his head. The story indicated that the murder was a random crime, and that Curtis was a homeless person. Finn noted the far-away look in Curtis's eyes labelled him as an obvious emotionally disturbed person, which was a clinical way of saying "nuts." Finn also made a mental note to keep his guard up if he ever ran into the homeless lady on Cross Bay Blvd. again.

Finn slid the newspaper back to Kevin. "What a shame. What are the odds that she would run into that nut?"

Kevin place marked something on the page with his right index finger. "This is all the evidence I need to convict this creep."

"What?"

"Three names, "Kevin responded.

"Come again?" Finn questioned.

"The mope has three names – Bobby Lee Curtis – anyone who uses three names is usually a killer."

"Brilliant deduction." Finn finished the last of the coffee from his cup.

GOODBYE GLADYS?

NOVEMEBER 4th - Finn entered the quiet of the pub with his phone already at his ear. He nodded to Kevin as he eased onto a stool at the empty bar but continued to direct his attention to the phone.

"So, how's this big case going Fineous?" Patrick's greeting indicated he had seen the caller information on his phone

"It's going nowhere," Finn responded, looking for an opening to get to his agenda.

Patrick expressed empathy. "That's where many of them go lad. It's the nature of the business."

"I know, but it's frustrating." Finn had his hook. "You know what else is frustrating, dad?"

"What?"

"Gladys!" Finn heard muffled laughter from the phone. "I'm glad you think this is funny."

"I know, Fineous, but she's an old woman. Have some sympathy and patience."

"Hey, dad, I'm one of the world's greatest sympathizers, but there are limits to everyone's patience."

"Come on now, Fineous, she can't be that bad."

"Oh no? The only time she's not late is when she doesn't show up at all. Half the time she's here she's asleep at her desk and the other half of the time she's knitting."

"Alright, Fineous."

"I'm not done yet, dad. When she does take a message, it's either a wrong or incomplete phone number, and I can't understand her handwriting."

“Don’t let her write messages then. Have her leave all her messages on the computer.” Patrick suggested.

The volume of Finn’s response distracted Kevin from his coffee making.

“SHE DOESN’T KNOW HOW TO USE A COMPUTER!”

“Calm down, lad,” Patrick cautioned.

Finn lowered his decibel level. “Sorry, dad. But I don’t think a worse secretary exists in the world – she has to go!”

“Really, Fineous?”

“You want me to build a successful business, right?”

“Of course!” Patrick shot back.

“Then Gladys has to go!”

“Then fire her.” Patrick said nonchalantly.

The pub was silent. Finn stared out the window to Woodhaven Blvd, phone still stuck to his ear.

“Fineous?” Patrick tried to confirm he was still on the line. When Finn finally responded, Patrick recognized the tone. It was the same tone his son used fifteen years earlier in explaining how he broke the living room window with a baseball.

“Uh, I can’t do that, dad. I’m not heartless.”

“Well what do you want me to do, Fineous?”

The life was back in Finn’s voice. “You fire her.”

“What?”

“That’s right!” Finn had found some momentum. “You gave her to me. It’s only right that you get rid of her!”

Finn detected a deep breath from the other end of the phone.

"Alright. I'll take care of it. Is she working tomorrow?" Patrick asked.

"Yes, at least she's scheduled to work," Finn corrected.

"Ok, I'll be at the office at 4:30 tomorrow afternoon."

"Thanks, dad."

"Now, Fineous, what were you saying about the big case?

"I was saying how frustrating it is."

"How so Fineous?"

Finn brought his dad up to date on his meetings with Susan Garland and Detective Don McHugh. His frustration was obvious when he reached the subject of Detective Delvecchio.

"I can't figure out why the Intelligence Division would be taking an interest in a simple missing persons case that may not even be a missing person. And now there's another Intel. Detective involved. It just doesn't make any sense."

"What's the other detective's name?" Patrick asked.

"Stanislas Karpinski."

"Stanislas Karpinski?" Patrick sounded puzzled. "I know a Stanislas Karpinski, but he's not a detective – he's a cop, and he worked patrol in Housing PSA 4."

"Then what…" Patrick cut Finn off.

"I'm not done yet, Fineous. This Stanislas Kaprinski retired six months ago."

There was silence over the phone line again until Finn vocalized a question.

"Could there be another Stanislas Karpinski on the job?"

"I sincerely doubt it, Fineous. But I'll check it out."

Finn put his iPhone on the bar.

"You sound like you could use a little extra zest today." Kevin put the hot cup of coffee in front of Finn and pointed to the Bailey's.

"No thanks – your magnificent coffee is enough medicine for me."

Finn savored his first sip while Kevin spiked his own cup with Bailey's.

"Hey Finn," Kevin said. "If you do fire that old battle axe, maybe I can work for you. What do you think?"

Finn put his coffee cup down, his mouth and eyes wide open.

"What's wrong with you?" Kevin responded.

"Oh my God!" Finn sounded frantic. "I have to call my dad back and apologize for lying to him."

"What are you talking about?"

"I told him that there couldn't possibly be a worse secretary in the world."

Finn sipped his coffee – totally satisfied with his zinger at Kevin, especially with the memory of Kevin's father's unfortunate fingers still fresh.

"Very funny, Finbar. Very Funny."

A BREAK FOR THANSGIVING

NOVEMBER 19th - Finn sat at his desk, doodling on a legal pad. It suddenly occurred to him that he wasn't in as much discomfort as was usual while seated in his horrendous chair. Was he finally breaking the chair in or was this simply his body's defense mechanism to help him tolerate the discomfort.

He looked at the clock on the wall above Gladys's empty desk – 3:15 PM. Doug Patterson was already fifteen minutes late for their appointment.

It had been over two weeks since his father agreed to fire Gladys, but legitimate or not, there had been one excuse after another preventing Patrick from performing the unpleasant duty.

Finn continued making his random circles and squares. Maybe the client's lateness was an omen that he shouldn't take a case on Thanksgiving, but the money he was offering was just too good to pass up. Finn had planned to use the holiday as a time be with his family, and most importantly, to clear his head of the Chelsea Garland case for at least one full day.

Other than identifying himself as the vice president of Atlas Foods, and specifying the attractive fee he was offering, Mr. Patterson had been very cryptic regarding the exact nature of the assignment, offering to explain the details fully at their meeting. Finn hoped this was a legitimate offer, and not just another crazy client to join his long line of screwballs.

The familiar sounds from the stairwell announced Doug Patterson's arrival. Finn's initial impression was positive. He certainly didn't look like a screwball. With his conservative business suit and haircut, the forty-something Doug Patterson looked every inch the corporate executive.

Finn had already pulled over the comfortable chair next to his desk, and Doug Patterson offered no apologies for his tardiness as he got right into the details of the assignment.

"As I mentioned in our phone conversation, Mr. Delaney, this is a one-day assignment that has to be performed in three days – on Thanksgiving."

"Understood," Finn responded.

"Are you familiar with Jackson Heights, Mr. Delaney?"

"Of course." Finn found the question somewhat odd considering that Jackson Heights was a Queens neighborhood located only two miles from where they were sitting.

"Have you ever heard of a Thanksgiving Ragamuffin Parade?"

"I can't say that I have." Finn responded.

"Well, let me give you a little history. This long-forgotten custom began in New York City sometime during the 1870s and was common in many urban areas throughout the remainder of the 19th century. Children would band themselves into a fantastically arrayed army of beggars and celebrate Thanksgiving by asking alms from adult pedestrians. Like Halloween, the youth that roamed the streets on Thanksgiving were prone to a great deal of mischief, especially if you didn't meet their demands by giving them either pennies, apples or candy. Adults increasingly grew tired of this tomfoolery occurring on Thanksgiving and by the 1950's, the tradition was on its way out. As the Thanksgiving Day Parade became the more recognized Thanksgiving tradition and celebration, the Ragamuffins slowly went away."

Finn held up his hand and shook his head. "I'm sorry, Mr. Patterson, but you lost me."

Doug Patterson returned the hand up gesture. "Let me finish. The tradition didn't fully die, however. Some neighborhoods held Ragamuffin parades as late as 1967, but now Jackson Heights is about to go old school with its own Thanksgiving Ragamuffin parade."

Finn was still clueless. "And why is this tradition important to me?"

Doug Patterson handed Finn his business card. "The Jackson Heights Civic Association has contracted Atlas Foods to be the exclusive food vendor for the event. My company has paid a substantial amount of money for these rights and we intend to protect our investment."

"I'm sorry, Mr. Patterson, but I still don't understand what you're driving at."

"Have you ever gone to a parade or street fair in Jackson Heights?" Patterson asked.

"I don't think so."

"Well," Patterson continued, "The streets are lined with illegal vendors, including food vendors. It's a problem everywhere in the city, but they seem to come out of the woodwork from everywhere in Jackson Heights."

Finn was beginning to get the picture. "I think I get it now, but what do you want me to do to stop these illegal food vendors?"

"Not stop them, Mr. Delaney – Record them. A strategy Atlas Foods has been successful with in other areas is to thoroughly document the illegal activities of these vendors, and then to drive them away from any future meddling through relentless litigation."

"Interesting," Finn opined.

"In order for this strategy to be effective," Patterson explained, "You need to get up really close to these vendors and video everything – who they are; what they're selling; any signs or other forms of identification."

Finn was back to being confused. "This seems like a pretty straightforward assignment, Mr. Patterson, but how am I going to be able to get close to these guys to record them?"

Doug Patterson smiled. "Don't worry, I have that all figured out. The parade runs for about a mile on 34th Avenue and 79th Street before terminating in the school yard of Our Lady of Fatima Catholic School. You and your associate will walk the parade route recording significant activities along the way."

Finn's eyes widened. "Associate?"

"Yes, you'll need to bring one of your investigators. This is a two-man job."

Doug Patterson stood up and extended his hand. "There's a White Castle restaurant on 88th Street and Northern Blvd. That's a couple of blocks from the beginning of the parade route. Meet me in the parking lot at 9 AM and I'll set you guys up."

Finn broke the handshake but still required more details. "Any particular specs for the video you require?"

"Don't worry about cameras," Patterson responded. "I'm supplying your entire set up."

"Ok, great." Finn nodded, curious about what the entire "set up" might entail.

Doug Patterson turned once more before entering the stairwell. "Ok, see you guys on Thursday morning."

"I'll.....," Finn caught himself. "We'll be there."

Finn returned to his doodling. He knew what had to be done, but he didn't want to do it. He had to find someone quick to work with him on Thanksgiving, and the reality of where he could find someone on such short notice was disturbing. Finn put the pen down on his doodling pad and left the office to perform his recruiting duties.

"Well, well! If it isn't another late afternoon appearance from New York City's favorite private dick." Kevin Malone cracked himself up more than any of the hand full of drinkers sitting at the bar.

Finn hopped up on a stool. "When you have a minute, I have to talk to you."

Kevin threw up his arms. "What did I do now?"

Finn waved his hand. "Nothing, nothing! I'm in a tough spot and I need for you to help me on a job."

"A job?" Kevin sang. "Just one minute."

Kevin refilled all the glasses on the bar whether they needed replenishment or not. He walked over to the empty corner and motioned to Finn. "Step into my office."

With the explanation completed, Finn waited for a response.

"Of course, I'll help you, buddy. What kind of a friend would I be otherwise?" Kevin's voice softened. "You are going to pay me, right?"

"Of course, good friend." Finn hoped the sarcastic tone wasn't lost on Kevin.

"I'll pick you up Thursday at 8AM. Be up or I swear I'll knock down your door." Finn eased himself off the stool.

"Don't worry, I'll be ready," Kevin said.

"Good, I'm out of here." Finn headed for the door.

"Oh, that's right," Kevin called to him. "Get out of here before SHE arrives."

"Asshole!" Finn sneered as he hit the door. On the sidewalk, he took a deep breath and sighed. His moron friend was actually right. He was consciously running from Meghan – Why?

THANKSGIVING DAY - Finbar Delaney Investigations Inc. was not a popular business in the Delaney household on Thanksgiving morning. Finn's older sister, her husband, and their three kids had come up from North Carolina, and Finn's mother was blowing a gasket at the prospect of Finn going to work on Thanksgiving. Molly Delaney had dealt with enough holidays without her husband present, and now her only son, even though he was no longer on the NYPD, was about to run off on Thanksgiving morning. Finn knew full well what his mom's response would be, which is why he waited to spring the news on her. With a promise to be back by dinner time, Finn was out the door.

Finn and Kevin relaxed in the Toyota, sipping cups of White Castle coffee.

"This is pretty good coffee," Finn commented.

Kevin shot back, "Not as good as mine, right?"

"Of course not!" Finn rolled his eyes.

Kevin flipped through the Daily News. "Hey, there is justice is the world after all."

"What are you talking about?" Finn asked.

Kevin pointed to an article. "Good old Billy Bob Dirtbag."

"Who?"

"The mope with the three names who did that sweet girl." Kevin simulated a gun with his thumb and index finger. "Two to the head – pop – pop."

"What about him?" As usual, Finn didn't understand his friend.

"He hung himself in his jail cell. Saved everyone a lot of time and money."

A white Atlas Foods van pulled into the parking lot.

"I wonder if that's him," Kevin said

"Wow, you were born for this business. What powers of observation," Finn chuckled.

"Happy Thanksgiving, men." Doug Patterson walked directly to the back of the van and opened the doors. Obviously, he wanted to get right to work. He pulled a large cardboard box out of the van and handed it to Finn.

"This is for you."

Finn placed the box on the ground and examined the contents. It looked like some kind of costume. His face quickly assumed the look of someone who was about to vomit. "Is this a costume?

"Of course," Patterson responded. "In a parade full of people in costumes, how else did you think you would be able to get close to these vendors?"

Finn shrugged and began rummaging through the box. "What is it?"

"You're a pilgrim," Patterson responded.

Finn was stunned. The costume was complete with a black coat with round silver button closures, a white falling band, and white cuffs at the wrists. There was also matching lightweight black knee-length breeches, and a broad-brimmed, high-crowned black hat with a gold buckle on the band. The costume also included an over-sized black vinyl belt worn over the jacket with an oversized brass buckle in the front. Rounding out this traditional pilgrim were knee-length white opaque stockings and gold shoe buckles with black faux leather tongues. As the finishing touches, Patterson reached further into the van and hand Finn a large musket and a small hatchet to tuck inside his belt.

Finn stood silently with his mouth wide open. He was speechless. Kevin, on the other hand, was almost falling over in delight.

"You're gonna look great, brother!" Kevin staggered and tried to keep his composure.

A second box produced by Patterson ended Kevin's merriment.

"This is for you."

"What?" Kevin muttered as he accepted the box.

The pilgrim wasn't as stunning as this costume. The turkey had a large, chocolate brown fur head with a big orange-yellow cloth beak and a large, long red wattle hanging down from the beak. The head was very large with big, blue and white cartoon-style plastic eyes. Including Kevin's own dimensions, the size of the head gave the turkey a height of about eight feet. Patterson pointed out that Kevin would be able to see through eye openings in the base of the neck, with the head and most of the neck being a detachable piece. The body featured matching brown fur with a colorful fur turkey tail attached to the back of the suit. The final touches included matching long fur dark brown mittens and large fur thigh-high boots.

Kevin was very clear in his assessment of the costume. "You're out of your mind, pal, if you think I'm gonna be walking around in this get-up."

Doug Patterson did not seem amused. "Mr. Delaney, you agreed to this assignment and I expect you to fulfill your part of the contract."

"It's OK, Mr. Patterson, just give me a minute." Finn pulled Kevin by the arm around the side of the van, his tone low enough so Patterson could not hear. "Look, there's no time to debate. You owe me about a million times over, so you're getting into that turkey suit."

Finn had miscalculated his volume, evidenced by Patterson's call to Kevin from the other side of the van.

"Stop wasting time and get into the costume like your boss is telling you."

Kevin bit his lip. He looked toward the direction of the orders and then back to Finn. "Yeah, sure. I'll wear the costume. No problem old buddy."

Doug Patterson had a few more instructions before Finn and Kevin suited up. "There are covert 1080P HD video cameras built into the belt buckle of the pilgrim and the chest of the turkey. Once you turn them on you have four hours of recording – more than enough for our purposes. Once the parade starts, just run around and entertain the kids, but make sure you get good close-up shots of all the food vendors lining the streets."

"Anything you say, boss." Kevin starting walking away

"Where do you think you're going?" Patterson barked.

"I gotta take a leak. Is that OK with you?" Kevin sneered as he pointed toward White Castle.

Five minutes later Kevin was back from the restaurant and a pilgrim and a turkey were now the prominent figures in the White Castle parking lot.

Doug Patterson activated both cameras. "You guys look great. Now, let's walk over to the start of the parade route. The turkey tried to sarcastically salute Patterson, but his turkey arm could only get as high as the base of his neck.

The movement of costumed adults and children west on 34th Avenue signaled that the parade was beginning. Doug Patterson, without a costume, provided the final instructions. “I am going to walk behind you and keep a close eye on the activity with the food vendors.”

34th Avenue was lined with parade watchers, mostly parents with their small children who seemed to be delighted with the passing costumed characters. Finn’s immediate impression was that the only food vendors along the route appeared to be elderly pretzel vendors.

The turkey’s neck leaned in close to the pilgrim and whispered, “OK, pilgrim – I’m going all in on this nonsense, so let’s give the kid’s a show.”

“What?” the pilgrim responded, with no other choice but to follow the turkey’s lead.

The children at the curb line squealed with delight as the brightly colored cartoonish turkey ran in small circles while being pursued by the pilgrim. As Kevin trotted near a very large curbside gathering of small children. Finn pointed his musket at the fleeing turkey and yelled “BANG”. Kevin dropped to the ground and laid flat on his stomach in front of the applauding throng. He pulled his right arm in from the costume, removed a red bottle from his pants pocket and waited. The pilgrim approached the fallen turkey and knelt next to the fallen bird.

“Get up,” he whispered. “You’re gonna freak the kids out with a dead turkey laying in the street.

“Oh, sorry,” was Kevin’s uncharacteristically cooperative response as the turkey sprung to life. The kids shrieked with joy at the sight of the revitalized bird. The turkey performed a couple of bizarre dance steps before approaching the pilgrim.

"Gimme that!" The turkey arm reached out and grabbed the plastic hatchet from the pilgrim's belt.

"What the hell are you doing?" the pilgrim protested.

"Watch me," snickered the turkey while protecting the hatchet from the grabs of the pilgrim.

The turkey moved in front of the largest contingent of young children he could find. He waved the hatchet in his turkey hand and declared to the adoring crowd in as loud a voice as he could muster. "LET ATLAS FOODS PROVIDE YOUR THANKSGIVING TURKEY!" As the last word came out of his mouth, his right hand swung the hatchet across his turkey neck. At the same time, he released the neck and head piece from the rest of the costume, giving the appearance that the turkey had just sliced its own head off. In a final artistic touch, Kevin began squeezing the bottle of ketchup he had just copped from White Castle, causing a stream of what appeared to be blood to come spouting out of the turkey's now headless neck area. The children were still squealing, but now they were squeals of terror at the sight of a headless "Tom Turkey" running down the street while spraying blood from where his head had just been lopped off.

Doug Patterson was not amused. Not only wasn't he going to pay Finn, but he was going to contact the Department of State to try to get his PI license revoked for his outrageous and unprofessional behavior.

The short ride home was completed in total silence. Finn pulled to a stop in front of Kevin's apartment building, and Kevin hesitated before exiting the vehicle.

"Look, I'm sorry. I know I screwed up again and you're probably going to disown me as a friend."

Finn stared straight ahead and remained silent. The passenger door slammed shut, but before Finn could step on the gas, there was tapping on the passenger window. Finn opened the widow about a quarter of the way and Kevin looked into the open space.

"But that guy was a pompous ass, and you have to admit that was funny."

Finn tried not to smile. "Happy Thanksgiving!"

He pulled away from the curb relieved that he no longer needed to stifle his laugh.

HUDSON STREET

NOVEMBER 27th - Finn was very fortunate to find a parking space on Spring Street, around the corner from 315 Hudson Street. As he and his dad turned the corner side by side onto Hudson Street, Finn looked up and eyed the nine-story structure. The NYPD Internal Affairs Bureau was inside this 1960s era, non-descript commercial office building? He could add this fact to the growing list of information about the NYPD that he did not know.

The double elevator door slid open on the third floor requiring Finn and Patrick to step out into a small reception area. The receptionist behind the desk was not Finn's perception of a typical corporate receptionist. This receptionist had a gold NYPD detective shield dangling in front of him, supported by a chain around his neck. The detective appeared to be 40-45 years of age, wearing a blue suit. Finn knew very little of style, but even a fashion novice could tell that this was a custom cut expensive suit to pay proper homage to the detective's trim figure. The detective's salt and pepper hair was a perfect complement to the suit, meticulously styled to the point that Finn was certain even a hurricane force wind would not knock even a single hair out of place.

Finn remained silent while Patrick handled the introduction, NYPD shield already in hand and displayed. "Chief Delaney here to see Inspector Dunne."

At the sight of the chief's shield, Finn noticed an immediate shift in demeanor from somewhat apathetic to over the top accommodating. "Sure thing, Chief. I'll call the Inspector right now. Please have a seat."

The detective already had the phone to his ear as he pointed toward an array of four chairs lined up to the right of the reception desk. Finn and Patrick had just settled into their seats when the detective was off the phone. "Chief – Inspector Dunne is in a meeting, but he should be free in a few minutes. Can I get you coffee, water – something?"

Patrick shook his head in the negative as Finn marveled at how completely this well-coiffed detective was sucking up to his father. One other fact had not been lost to Finn. This detective was so intimidated by his dad's rank that he had never even asked who Finn was, or if he was even with his father.

Patrick and Finn waited in silence as the debonair detective returned to his receptionist duties. With the volume of his voice turned high, it was impossible for Finn not to eavesdrop on the detective's phone conversation.

"Hey, what's up dude? You work last night?

There was a momentary silence as the detective switched from talker to listener. Soon, however, he was back on the offensive.

"You're downstairs? Come on up bro. – I'm not busy."

Unless the wait terminated, Finn realized that the little group in the reception area would soon be joined by a cop friend of the detective. The bell signaled the arrival of the elevator on the third floor, and the response of the detective signaled the arrival of his visitor.

"Hey, hey, what's up my man?" The detective came out from behind his desk and greeted his visitor with a very manly handshake into a shoulder bump followed by a back slap. The new arrival was in the same age range but had a completely different look than the suave detective. His full head of brown hair was unkempt, and a red checkered flannel shirt did little to mask his ample girth. His belly hung over old looking blue jeans that terminated at equally well-worn dirty white sneakers.

Two cop buddies greeting each other. Nothing unusual here Finn thought. So, it was very puzzling when Patrick seemed to tense to attention and slap Finn's left knee.

"What?" Finn glanced toward his father.

Patrick said nothing, but slightly shook his head, a gesture Finn interpreted as an order to keep quiet.

"Chief, how are you?" The door to the inner offices had sprung open and Inspector Michael Dunne offered a traditional handshake to Patrick. As they were being ushered through the door Patrick introduced his son.

"Mike, this is my son Finbar. Fineous, this is Inspector Dunn."

Finn smiled as they exchanged hands. "It's a pleasure to meet you sir."

Finn heard something else besides his conversation with Inspector Dunne. Before they moved away from the reception area door, he thought he heard someone from outside say, "How are you, Chief?" and he was sure he heard his father say, "I'm good."

Inspector Dunne led them across the large cubicle filled room. Just as they reached Dunne's office, Patrick stopped in the doorway.

"Gimme a second, Mike. I'm just going to get some water."

Before he had an opportunity to enter the Inspector's office, Patrick gently grabbed Finn by the arm and guided him to the water cooler. As the water flowed, Patrick spoke quickly. “Don’t say anything about the case until I figure out what’s going on here.”

Finn was clueless. “What?”

Patrick took a big sip of water and threw the cup in the trash. “The guy who just showed up outside by the elevator.”

“Yeah?” Finn still had no idea of what his father meant.

“That was Stanislas Karpinski.”

Finn again whispered “What?”, but now it was a declaration of astonishment as opposed to ignorance.

“Just keep quiet,” Patrick warned as they returned to Inspector Dunne’s office. Finn had a notion that his dad was being strategic during the mandatory small talk period of the conversation.

“Wow, Mike, this is quite a set up here, complete with Rico Suave greeting us at the elevator.”

“Yeah,” Dunne chuckled. “Tony Defama really cuts a fine figure of a man, doesn’t he? Nothing but the best for Tony – finest suits, best cars, finest wine.”

“And he’s in IAB?” It was impossible to miss Patrick’s sarcasm.

“He’s legit.” Dunne countered. “I hear his family has money.”

Patrick nodded, and Dunne continued. “He also lucked into the ultimate side gig.”

Patrick leaned back and stroked his chin, in anticipation of an explanation.

“Do you know the Kelly brothers?”

Patrick went through his vast mental rolodex. "I don't think so."

"They're retired now. John worked for years in Narcotics and Jim was a detective in Intel. About ten years ago they opened a security company."

Finn decided to jump in. "What kind of security do they do?"

Patrick shot the look of an annoyed father at his disobedient son as Dunn continued.

"They only have one client. Through his work in Intel., years ago Jimmy got hooked up with the royal family of one of those small Middle Eastern countries. They're here so often, the king wanted a private security detail available all the time. They rent out two floors of a midtown luxury hotel and the Kelly's security company set up an actual security command center there. I've never seen it but I heard it looks like a miniature version of the war room at One Police Plaza." Inspector Dunne took a breath and continued. "The Kelly's hire only off duty and retired NYPD to staff the detail. The pay is great – about $60 an hour."

"That is great for a part time gig." Patrick opined.

"That's nothing," Dunne continued. "I heard that the crown prince of the family is a real party animal. He has his favorite crew of security people that are assigned to him. Tony Defama is one of the prince's favorites. The team looks out for him while he's in the city and he takes care of them."

"Takes care of them?"

"Yeah, I heard the prince comes here with suitcases filled with cash. The security team makes sure the prince is safe and doesn't run into any trouble, and in return I hear he is very generous to the team."

"How generous?"

"I'm an inspector in IAB. I don't care to know anymore.

Everyone laughed nervously, and the subject was dropped.

"So, what can I do for you Chief?"

Finn was very curious regarding the information on Defama and Karpinski, but he was just as curious to see how his dad was going to avoid talking about the case.

"You know what happened to my son. I was wondering if you knew anything about civilian investigator openings with the Civilian Complaint Review Board."

This is great, Finn thought. Just what he needed – another job set up by his father.

The car door slammed closed, filtering out most of the sounds of the city on Spring Street. Finn latched his seatbelt but made no move toward the engine start button. Patrick had just settled into the passenger seat and Finn turned toward his father.

"What do you think?"

"I don't really know, Fineous," Patrick answered in a slow measured pace, emphasizing his uncertainty. "This may be absolutely nothing, but there's some weird stuff going on here. I came here trying to find out something about Detective Delvecchio and why the Intelligence Division would be involved with your missing person. Out of the blue, Stanislas Karpinski walks into our world, and he appears to be best buds with detective fashion plate.

Top it off with the Kelly brothers and their lucrative security company and what do we have?

“I have absolutely no idea.” Finn declared as he pulled onto Spring Street.

“Neither do I.” Patrick laughed.

“Why didn’t you see what Inspector Dunne knew about Delvecchio?”

“Caution, Fineous, caution. Mike Dunne is probably alright, but there was just too much going on there with that Tony guy and Karpinski. I couldn’t take any chances.”

“By the way, dad, do you think you’ll ever get around to taking care of that business with Gladys?”

“Next week.”

“I’ve heard that before,” Finn blurted sarcastically.

“Next week – definitely!” Patrick’s agitation was clear.

PIE

NOVEMBER 28th - Finn pulled to a stop on the stretch of Cross Bay Blvd. that had become all too familiar to him. Similarly, as he turned the corner onto 12th street Finn experienced the all too familiar feeling of apprehension – apprehension at having to meet again with Susan Garland, provide her with virtually no new information, and deal with her emotional roller coaster ride. Why was he even meeting her in person? Couldn't he explain just as quickly on the phone that he had nothing new to report? As he approached the gate to the tiny front yard, Finn felt ashamed. He mouthed silently what had become his personal mantra, "Suck it up!" After all, it wasn't his daughter who was missing. Was it too much for him to attempt to provide some semblance of comfort to this woman in obvious distress?

The only sound was the ornate European clock on the living room wall. Finn was back in his usual position at the Mahogany table, facing Susan and articulating how his investigation had basically uncovered nothing. Finn immediately noticed a very different Susan Garland. This was not the emotional wreck he had met several days earlier. This Susan was completely devoid of emotion. Was she medicated or emotionally drained?

Again, the clock became the only audible sound. Susan sat across from Finn, hands cupped under her chin. She looked to the living room window and spoke in a voice barely above a whisper. "I have always loved the way the clouds drift by and the way the leaves move in a breeze with that soft whispering sound they make. Now, there is only a creeping sorrow where there should be joy. It sits like the November rain on my skin, enough to chill what was once warm inside. When this nightmare began, I called friends and asked for the warmth I needed to ward off the sorrow just a little bit." Susan moved her fingers to her temples and shook her head. "No longer - Now I just let the sorrow come, drop by drop, and now the grief has condensed above my head into a cloud large enough to block out the sun." Susan dropped her hands to the table and looked directly at Finn. "They say it can't rain forever, that there will come a time when the last drop has fallen. Thing is, I just don't care."

Finn breathed a huge sigh of relief as he closed the chain link gate behind him and headed in the direction of Cross Bay Blvd. His relief was short lived. He rolled his eyes and took a deep breath at the sight of the homeless woman perched on the corner of Cross Bay, directly in the path to his car.

He still had about four hundred feet to traverse, and as he drew closer Finn determined a strategy shift was in order. He would switch from direct engagement to total indifference. He would act as if the woman did not exist.

Finn was so totally focused on the woman and his strategy – he never saw them coming. Two males were crossing 12th Street and were rapidly approaching Finn.

"Hey!" The alert from one of the males did not sound friendly.

Finn's attention immediately snapped to his left. The unfriendly male continued in a similar tone. "Who the hell are you?"

Finn stopped in his tracks and tried to comprehend what was happening. He knew these men – but from where? The surly male was now face to face with him.

"Didn't you hear me? I asked who the hell you are"

Finn's ability to roll with the punches had it limits, and this pompous ass had pushed Finn across the line. "Who the hell are you?" he snapped back. Finn had no chance for any follow up question before a black leather case was flipped open and a gold NYPD detective shield was thrust to within a few inches of his eyes.

"Now, let's go through this one more time," the shield holder sarcastically stated. "Who the hell are you and what are you doing here?

"I'm a private investigator." As Finn responded he removed his New York State Private Investigators license from his wallet and offered it to the detective. The detective snatched the license roughly from Finn's grasp. He studied the license and continued his interrogation.

"So, Mr. Private Investigator, what are you doing here?"

"I was meeting with a client – a woman on the block whose daughter is missing. "Finn pointed in the general direction of Susan's house. Finn's annoyance level was rising. "Is there some problem here? I don't understand."

The detective stopped studying the license and extended it in his hand towards Finn. "The problem, my friend, is that you have no case here – drop it!"

"What?"

The agitation level of the detective rose noticeably. "Am I not speaking English? I said DROP IT!" To emphasize his point, he jabbed the edge of Finn's license into his forehead before dropping it on the sidewalk in front of him. "Oops. Sorry about that." The detective looked at his silent partner and they exchanged snickers.

Finn rubbed his forehead as he bent down to retrieve his license. Without another word he began his trek toward Cross Bay, his ego bruised much worse than his forehead. His greatest distress, however, was not physical. He still could not recall where he had seen those two detectives before.

Oh no! With all his attention focused on the interaction with the less than friendly policemen, Finn had almost forgotten about his homeless friend. As he approached the corner, he continued with his new strategy of disengagement. He passed the homeless woman and turned his head away, pretending that she didn't exist. He could hear her growling and hissing as he passed, but at least he didn't have to see her.

Finn paused outside his driver's door and fished through his pockets for his key fob. While that search was ongoing, a similar search was taking place in his mind. Who were those guys? He knew he had seen them before, but he just couldn't recall where. One search was resolved when his hand emerged from his right pants pocket, tightly gripping the key fob. Two quick tweets and the door opened. Finn pivoted to his right in anticipation of sliding into the driver's seat. Something caught his eye in the extreme edge of his peripheral vision. Finn gasped and stepped back. He was stunned. Standing no more than two feet from him was the homeless lady, silently glaring into his eyes. Finn was frozen as the woman sang in a guttural growl.

"How many pieces of pie can you eat when you're blind or dead?"

Finn remained silent as the woman sang her question in a louder growl.

"How many pieces of pie can you eat when you're blind or dead? Tell her!"

Finn began to regain some composure. “What? Tell who?”

The woman began a slow retreat while continuing her growl. “Tell her – tell her!”

Finn pulled away from the curb and stopped at the red light. He tapped the steering wheel before shouting out loud to himself, “What the hell was that?”

DECEMBER 2nd - The bullying detectives and crazy singing homeless lady had shaken Finn. He needed a few days removed from the Chelsea Garland case, and his increasing caseload of cheaters and other assorted kooks provided a good excuse to take a quick respite from bully cops, depressed mothers, and singing crazy ladies. It was stressful enough dealing with the emotional highs and lows of Susan Garland, but now he still had a mark on his forehead from the unsociable, cryptic detective, and he still had no idea what that crazy homeless lady was talking about with her pie eating rant. And who were these unfriendly detectives? It was nagging at him that he was sure he knew them but could not for the life of him remember where.

Finn leaned forward, resting his elbows on his desk, his left hand displaying the screen of his iPhone. For the past two days there seemed to be some invisible force preventing his right index finger from contacting the call icon. That force field had worn away, however. Good conscience would not allow him to go any further without checking in.

“Hello Susan, it’s Finn Delaney.”

“Hello Finn.” This was definitely the depressed version of Susan, but over the phone Finn could not determine if she was better or worse than their last meeting.

“I’m just checking in to see if there’s anything new.” Finn figured this was a better way to explain that he had absolutely no new information for her.

“No, there’s nothing new Finn.” Susan stated in a low, emotionless tone.

"Have you heard anything from the police?" Finn probed.

"Nothing new," Susan stated. "They still come by almost every day, though."

"They do?" Finn's curiosity was sparked. "When did they come by last?"

"A couple of hours ago. It's always the same. They want to know if I have heard from Chelsea."

Finn was still thinking of a follow up question when Susan continued.

"As a matter of fact, they came by a few minutes after your last visit. I'm surprised you didn't see them."

Finn unconsciously ran his left index finger over the mark still visible on his forehead. "Were those the same detectives who always come by?"

"Yes," Susan responded. "It was Delvecchio and ….."

"Karpinski!" Finn finished Susan's sentence for her. The light bulb had inexplicitly flipped on in his brain. That's why he looked so familiar to him. It was the same Stanislas Karpinski he had seen fist bumping with the best dressed detective at IAB headquarters.

"Do you know them?" Susan's voice contained just a hint of emotion.

"No." Finn reigned in his emotions. "I just remember the names from you telling me."

The detective mystery was partially solved, now it was time for Finn to address another, if he could remember it correctly. "Susan, this is going to sound very strange, but does this mean anything to you?"

"What?"

Finn was having trouble recalling the homeless lady's rant correctly. "Do you ever eat pie with sunglasses on?"

"What the hell are you talking about?" There was emotion in her voice, but that emotion was irritation. Finn kept fishing for the right words. After several additional attempts he finally got it.

"How many pieces of pie can you eat when you're blind or dead?"

Silence on the line – Finn's initial thought was that Susan had hung up on him. The silence was short-lived, as the other end of the line suddenly exploded with emotion.

"Oh my God! Oh my God! Where did you hear that? Who told you that?"

"Wait a minute, Susan. Tell me what it means." Finn could sense that Susan was having difficulty restraining her emotions.

Susan's response was better suited for the bleachers of a football stadium. "IT MEANS SHE'S ALIVE!"

"What?" Finn's jaw had dropped as far as humanly possible. "Please, help me understand this, Susan."

Susan's excited state was still obvious, but she seemed to have regained a degree of composure.

"When Chelsea was about nine years old, she began singing this little song. It was just a silly song that she made up. Whenever we would be driving someplace, I would hear her in the back seat singing 'how many pieces of pie can you eat when you're blindfolded.' I thought she was singing 'how many pieces of pie can you eat when you're blind or dead. It was such a ridiculous mistake that we still laugh about the horrible lines I thought she was singing."

Susan suddenly regained her sense of priority. "Tell me Finn, please, who said those words to you?"

Finn's brain was going in a million different directions. Had Susan finally broken free from reality? He needed time to digest these developments and seek counsel from his dad. "Susan, trust me. I can't say anything more right now, but I'll get back to you as soon as I get more information." Before ending the conversation, he had one more thought. "Susan, don't tell the police anything about this."

Finn leaned back in the uncomfortable chair, tapping a rhythm on the desktop while staring out to Woodhaven Blvd. There was still something nagging at him. He now knew that Delvecchio was the culprit of his forehead poke, but before the harassment on 12th Street, he was sure he had seen Delvecchio before,.- but where? Maybe it was all the information flowing freely in his brain that pushed one previously hidden fact into his consciousness. He jumped up from his uncomfortable seat. "That's it!" he declared to no one but himself as he pounded his fists on the desktop as an exclamation point to his declaration.

Halfway down the steps Finn had to ease up. In his excitement he was moving too fast and he could feel the tension in his right knee. Even with the twinge in his knee, Finn could not restrain himself from performing a combination run/walk/skip across the street. It was fortunate there was no one standing on the other side of the heavy wood door as Finn burst through. He paid no attention to the clientele at the bar as he demanded Kevin's attention.

"Hey! What day were we looking at the paper?"

Kevin held up his hands, surprised at Finn's frantic tone. "Whoa! Easy partner. What the hell are you talking about?"

Finn would not be restrained. "The newspaper – the Post, I think."

"What about the Post?" Kevin was still clueless.

"Come on." Finn had no patience, but he suddenly understood how he could reach Kevin's level of understanding. "We were reading the story about the killer with the three names – remember?"

"Oh yeah," Kevin responded. "The creep who killed that hot girl, right?"

"That's it!" Finn pounded his fist on the bar.

"So?" Kevin still didn't understand the significance of the revelation.

"What day were we looking at that story?"

Kevin peered out to Woodhaven Blvd. "Hmm – I don't know – three or four weeks ago, maybe. What's your point, private eye?"

Finn disregarded Kevin's question. "Do you still have that newspaper?"

"Of course," Kevin stated. "I make paper hats and party favors from all the old newspapers. What are you – nuts? We don't store old newspapers."

Finn paid no mind to the sarcastic shot. He hopped on a stool and pulled out his iPhone. "I just hope their website gives access to recently archived editions."

Kevin didn't know what to think. He began to refill glasses of impatient drinkers while trying to figure out if his friend had lost his mind. Finn continued to work feverishly on the screen of his phone while verbalizing each move.

"OK, I got the right date – now, if I can only find the photo."

Kevin was still catching up with his drink backlog when his concentration was broken by Finn's shout.

"Holy shit!"

Finn held up the phone and excitedly waved Kevin over. "Look – look at this!" Finn handed the phone to Kevin.

Kevin still didn't understand the significance. "OK, it's a photo of Billy Bob Creep, or whatever his name is."

Finn snatched the phone back. "Not the creep. The cops – the detective on the creep's right."

Kevin took the phone for another look and then returned the device to Finn. "Yeah, that certainly is a detective on the creep's right. I think you need some sleep, Finbar."

Finn held the phone up and pointed to the screen. "That guy on the right."

"Yeah?" Kevin responded with mock anticipation.

"That guy did this!" Finn dramatically moved his finger from the screen to his forehead, pointing to the mark from the poke of his PI license.

Kevin passed out a fresh beer to the end of the bar. "You're still not speaking English, bro."

Finn reset himself on the stool and took a deep breath. Maybe he had been a bit too excited. "The detective from the Intelligence Division who is involved with this case for some reason – Delvecchio – he's the guy who poked me in the forehead and told me not to come back."

Finn pointed to his phone again. "That's Delvecchio escorting the killer of Cynthia Dubois."

"So?" Kevin repeated. "Detective's work a lot of cases. What's so weird about that?"

Finn put his phone on the bar and held up one hand. "I know this is hard for you – but try to think! Chelsea Garland goes missing on October 1st. On the same night, Cynthia Dubois is found in the dumpster. The same detective is involved in both cases, and the detective is from the Intelligence Division? Something is not right here. And why would Delvecchio care if I was working for Susan Garland?"

Kevin leaned across the bar with an astonished look on his face. "Oh my God – I get it now. Do you want my advice?"

"Of course." Finn picked up his phone and sat up straight.

"Drink heavily!"

Finn hopped off the stool and headed for the door. "When will I ever learn!"

A CHRISTMAS GIFT

DECEMBER 3rd - Patrick Delaney stretched his arms and yawned in the reclined easy chair. He folded his arms as the chair returned to the upright position. Patrick got up and took a lap around the living room before replanting himself in his favorite chair.

"It's no fun getting old, Fineous."

Finn had less than zero interest in his father's aging tribulations. "What do you think, dad?"

Patrick nodded. "There certainly are some very strange facts in your story, and I don't like that Delvecchio character making veiled threats to you. I have a good mind to call him downtown and read him the riot act."

"Please don't," Finn pled. "If you come down on him, that might end everything."

Patrick smiled. "You're starting to get into this, aren't you, Fineous?"

"Maybe," Finn shrugged. "The mother may have gone off the deep end with the pie song, but for the first time I'm beginning to believe that I may actually be able to bring closure to this case – good or bad."

Patrick continued to nod. I know the feeling, Fineous. It's your curious mind – your need to know."

Patrick Delaney seemed momentarily lost in the moment, as if waging a battle with his feelings – good feelings of watching his son work the investigation and bad feelings at thinking about what could have been.

Finn brought his dad back to the problem at hand. "Well, what do you think I should do?"

"You need to get information on the arrest of the Cynthia Dubois perpetrator, and try to see how Delvecchio and the Intelligence Division figure in to this."

"How am I going to do that?" Finn asked. "Do I just walk into the precinct?"

Patrick beckoned with his right hand. "Let me see that picture of the arrest in the 7th Precinct again."

Finn produced his phone, tapped on the screen furiously for thirty seconds, and handed the device to his dad. Patrick took a long look at the photo. "The guy on the left is Billy Johnson from the 7th Precinct Squad. I'll call him."

"You're going to make an appointment for me?" Finn questioned.

"No, Fineous, the situation is getting a bit dicey and this is a murder. I'll talk to him."

"When are you going to call him?" Finn continued.

"There's no time like the present." Patrick snatched back Finn's phone.

Patrick flipped thumbs up when the police administrative aide confirmed that Detective Johnson was present in the station house.

"Chief Delaney, how are you. Long time no-speak." On the speaker, Finn detected apprehension in Detective Johnson's voice.

"I'm good, Billy." Like most cop conversations, Patrick embarked on the obligatory trip down memory lane with tales of mutual acquaintances and where they work, or if they retired, or when they passed away. With the mandatory preliminaries taken care of Patrick pushed forward.

"Hey Billy, I see you made a collar on the dumpster murder."

"Yeah Chief, I got that one cleared. A local homeless guy popped her – two in the head."

"How did you tie her to that homeless mutt?"

"We got this guy good, Chief. I got the gun on the guy, and the mope confessed."

"Really?" Patrick stated. "How did you get turned on to him as a suspect?"

"Like a gift-wrapped present on Christmas morning, Chief."

"What do you mean?" Patrick chuckled.

"I have to be honest – I had nothing going on the case – no leads. Then one-day Santa walks into the station house with a present."

"What?"

"Out of the blue, this Detective from Intel. comes walking in with this mutt in tow. He gives me the mutt, the gun, and the confession – Merry Christmas."

"How the hell did Intel. get on this?"

"He said something about some investigation they were on in the area, but I didn't really care." Johnson said.

"You don't find it odd, Billy, that Intel. picked up a homeless guy off the street." Patrick asked.

"Odd? Who cares- the case was cleared. And even if I wanted to dig deeper the mope did everyone a favor by hanging himself in his jail cell. Happy ending for everyone, right?"

"Yeah Billy, a really happy ending," Patrick's response was unenthusiastic.

When the call was over, Patrick handed the phone back to Finn. "I don't like what I'm hearing Fineous."

Finn was afraid his dad was going to shut him down and take matters into his own hands. "Look, dad, I'm not going to get involved with Delvecchio or any other cops. I just need to follow up with the homeless lady and Susan Garland – OK?"

Patrick bit his lip. "OK Fineous, you keep working your case. But you have to do me one favor right now."

"Sure, what?"

"Activate the phone locate feature on your iPhone."

"OK, but why?" Finn questioned.

"If you ever run into any problems," Patrick cautioned, "911 text me and I'll get to you as soon as is possible."

"Sounds good," Finn stated as he activated the feature.

"And Fineous, I'm coming by the office tomorrow afternoon to take care of the Gladys business – definitely!"

AN UNLIKELY SAVIOR

DECEMBER 4th - It was 10:30 AM, and as had become the norm, Finn sat alone in the office reviewing his case files. Where was Gladys? Who knew? And at this point, who cared? Certainly not Finn. He did hope that she materialized sometime during the day. This was "G" day – the day his dad had promised to lower the boom, but there could be no "G" day without Gladys.

At 10:50 Finn recognized the familiar sounds coming from the stairway. Gladys would be making her appearance in five to ten minutes. Activity at the office entrance entered Finn's peripheral vision. Wow! Gladys must have taken a vitamin today and sprinted up the stairs. When Finn's head turned toward the activity, it was clear that it wasn't Gladys who had sprinted up the steps. A bald man in a tan winter overcoat and tie walked toward Finn, business card extended in his hand.

"I'm looking for Finbar Delaney."

"That's me." Finn stood and accepted the card.

MICHAEL J. RAMSEY

LICENSE INVESTIGATOR

NEW YORK STATE DEPARTMENT OF STATE

"What can I do for you, Mr. Ramsey?" Finn knew immediately what this was about. This state investigator was here as a result of the Thanksgiving Day fiasco. Finn's blood was boiling, but he wasn't sure who to direct his anger at – that prick Doug Patterson, or his moron friend Kevin. Finn quickly decided he had enough anger inside him to go around to both.

Michael Ramsey spoke very officiously. "I'm here investigating allegations that you took actions during an investigation that are in contravention to the rules and regulations of a New York State Private Investigator."

Finn took a deep breath. With no preparation he commenced a speech that he hoped would save his business. Approximately twenty minutes after the interrogation began, Finn believed he was doing well. He tried to sum up like a lawyer making a closing statement at a trial. "So, you see, Mr. Ramsey, this whole episode was basically one big misunderstanding. My investigator and I believed we had a two-pronged responsibility. We knew we were supposed to gather the video evidence regarding the illegal street vendors, but we were also under the impression that we were supposed to really perform a show on the street. After all, we were provided these elaborate costumes and props."

Finn had no idea if Ramsey was buying his line of bullshit, but he wasn't going to stop now. "For the performance part of the assignment, we weren't given any script, so we improvised with the costumes and equipment we had. I admit we did miscalculate the audience. We didn't realize the large number of small children present or we would never had performed the turkey decapitation scene." Finn did his best to look contrite. "But for an adult audience, that routine is darkly humorous, don't you think?"

"Well, that's debatable." Ramsey looked up from his notes. "But it's not beyond the scope of reasonable behavior."

Finn breathed a big sigh of relief. He had done it. He had talked the life back into his business. Mr. Ramsey turned the page on his notebook. "Now I just need a few documents for the audit. Audit? Finn's spirits sank. What audit?

"An audit?" Finn asked, hoping maybe he hadn't heard Ramsey correctly.

"Yes. An audit is a standard part of all investigations – strictly routine."

Well, this may have been routine for Michael Ramsey, but besides the private investigator license hanging on the wall, Finn wasn't really sure if he could locate any of the documents New York State required him to maintain. As a matter of fact, he wasn't even sure if he was maintaining all the required records.

Finn was beginning to feel ill. "What records do you need to see?"

"Just some very basic documents." Ramsey paged through his notebook. Finn's spirits were on the upswing. Maybe this wouldn't be so bad. Ramsey settled on a page in his book. "I need to see copies of all your written contracts for every investigative assignment; proof of insurance, and a copy of your current surety bond. I also need to see copies of all your investigative employee documents."

Finn perked up. "I don't have any investigative employees."

Ramsey looked up from his notebook and frowned. "You don't? What about the investigator who worked with you on Thanksgiving?"

Finn's spirits plummeted to new depths. He was hardly listening to Ramsey. What was the use.

"I need copies of employee statements, requests for fingerprints, and copies of fingerprint cards. I also need copies of required employee ID cards that meet Department of State specifications."

Finn rubbed his forehead. "Let me see what I can find, Mr. Ramsey. My secretary is off today."

The Hail Mary attempt of the secretary being off fell incomplete with the sounds of activity in the stairway. Oh, no, did she have to show up now. Finn turned and looked out the window, tapping his fingers on his desk. This was his version of a white flag. He had surrendered.

Five minutes of finger tapping elapsed before Ramsey intervened. "Excuse me, Mr. Delaney – the documents?"

Finn turned from the window and smiled. "Oh, I'm sorry. Mr. Ramsey, my secretary will be here momentarily."

Gladys Kowalski emerged for the stairway huffing through a string of complaints. "It's too damn cold to be coming out of the house. It's tough enough making it up these stairs, no less in a heavy coat."

Gladys took off her coat and unloaded her usual supplies on her desk. Finn was perversely amused by the thought of the scene he knew was about to unfold.

"Good morning, Gladys," Finn sung in an over the top happy voice.

Gladys looked up and pointed to Ramsey. "Who's this?"

Finn maintained his fake elation. "Why, this is Mr. Ramsey from the Department of State."

"What does he want?" Gladys sneered.

"Not much," Finn sang. "Just a few little documents he needs for his audit. Why don't you tell Gladys what you need, Mr. Ramsey?" Finn walked to the window as Ramsey went through his list again. The executioner was at the door. Finn smirked. At least he would be able to get rid of that stupid sign. The feeling of illness had overtaken Finn again. "I'll be back in a minute. I just need a little air."

Finn leaned against the lamppost and watched the traffic fly by on Woodhaven Blvd. He looked up to his office windows and to the ridiculous sign. Finned wondered if he really could have made a go of it as a private eye. He would never find out. Oh well, it was time to face the music.

Finn entered the office to see Michael Ramsey closing his briefcase. Ramsey turned and extended his hand. He appeared substantially more at ease. "Thanks Mr. Delaney. I have everything I need."

"You do?" Finn questioned.

"Yes, and I must say, Mr. Delaney that it is a pleasure to deal with a company that has their administrative records in such good order."

"It is?" Finn didn't know what to say, so he said nothing more.

Finn peeked out the window to make sure Ramsey was gone. "What just happened here, Gladys?"

Gladys already had her knitting needles out. "What are you talking about? The man asked for some records and I gave them to him."

"You had all the records?" Finn could not believe it was possible.

"Are you OK, Finn?" Gladys put down the needles. "You gave me a copy of the State licensing law when I started working here, and you said that all the records I needed to maintain were in the book."

"And you actually read that book?"

"You're funny, Finn." Gladys chuckled and picked up her knitting needles.

Finn still could not believe what happened. "Wait a minute Gladys. How come I've never seen you working on these documents?"

Gladys put down the needles again. She seemed annoyed. "What do you think I'm doing while you're sitting on a bar stool across the street?"

Finn's curiosity was still not satisfied. "What about the employee documents? You had records for Kevin?

"Of course."

"What about fingerprints? You never took his prints."

Gladys looked indignant. "Excuse me. I most certainly did fingerprint your friend. As soon as you told me he was going to work with you on Thanksgiving, I called him and told him to come by, so I could fingerprint him and make an ID card for him."

"You're really on the level, Gladys?"

"I'm starting to feel insulted Finn. Not only did I make his ID card, but if you check it you will see that it is made exactly according to New York State specifications."

"I'm sorry, Gladys." Finn leaned over and gave her a peck on the cheek.

"What's that for Finn?"

"For being the best secretary, a boss could ask for."

Finn spent the rest of the day stunned. At 4:00 he decided to drift across the street. Kevin was busy with the normal afternoon drinkers, so Finn made a detour before the bar.

"Starting early today, huh?"

Meghan spun around from the hostess podium, her eyes lit up like candles.

"Oh, Hi, Finn. Yeah. I had to start at 4:00 today. How was your Thanksgiving?"

Meg nearly fell over in laughter as Finn related the tale of the headless Thanksgiving turkey. Why the heck had he been avoiding Meg? He felt so comfortable talking to her. His innate social awkwardness, however, was preventing him from taking the next step.

"I gotta go see my lunatic friend over there." Finn pointed to the bar.

"Stop by before you leave." Meg requested

"Sure!" Finn smiled all the way to the bar.

Finn's smile paled compared to Kevin's. "I knew you would eventually make your move Romeo!"

"Just shut up for a minute. I have an important question. Do you have an ID card from my company?"

Kevin dug into his back pocket and produced his wallet. He flipped open his wallet and pulled out a card. He held the card up next to his face. "Good picture, don't you think?"

Finn was flabbergasted. "When did you get that card?"

"That old bat of yours called me the day before Thanksgiving and told me to get my ass up there for an ID card or I wouldn't be able to work."

“Really?” Finn was only now completely believing what had happened. His secretary actually was a secretary.

“Hey Finn” Kevin was peering out the window. “Isn’t that your dad’s car across the street? Tell him to stop in and say hello.”

Finn’s right knee buckled slightly as he hopped off the stool and began moving for the door as quickly as possible. He didn’t notice the sad look on Meg’s face as he flew past her without acknowledgement. Finn pulled himself up the handrails, hopping up the steps on his left leg. Finn burst into the office, huffing and puffing from his unexpected sprint.

“Hey, Fineous, where’s the fire?” Patrick joked at seeing the condition of his son.

Finn placed his hands on his hips, still trying to catch his breath. Patrick brought Finn up to date. “I just started having a conversation with Gladys. I was telling her that all companies evolve and make changes.”

“Most companies do.” Finn was finally able to talk. “But not this company. We’re not ready for any changes yet. We’re working as well as we possibly can just the way we are.”

“Really?” Patrick was trying to figure out what was going on.

“Really!” Finn emphasized. “Kevin was just asking for you. Why don’t you go across the street and say hello. And while you’re at it, ask to see his ID card.”

Finn began guiding Patrick toward the stairs. “Yeah, Kevin’s dying to see you. I’ll come by when I finish up here.”

Halfway down the stairs a very confused Patrick Delaney stopped and called out. “Fineous!”

Finn stuck his head into the stairway.

“Is everything alright?” Patrick questioned.

Finn smiled. “Everything’s perfect!”

THE SECOND FRONT

DECEMBER 5th - For several months Finn's normal experience at The Shamrock had been his intimate conversations with Kevin over coffee and a newspaper in the solitude of the late morning empty bar. With his buddy covering for one of the regular night bartenders, Finn decided to revisit the evening scene. At 9 PM on Friday night the pub was a symphony of conversations told in loud voices, all of them competing with the rock music that dominated the atmosphere. The crowd was young, mostly members of several student organizations from nearby Molloy College. There was also the unmistakable presence of a contingent of off duty cops segregated into one corner of the bar.

Finn wedged into an empty spot at the bar, put down a twenty-dollar bill, and patiently waited. Kevin and the other bartender were performing a frantic, non-stop dance that seemed to keep time with the pulsating music. Finn wasn't sure if Kevin had noticed his presence, but the appearance of a bottle of Coors Light next to his still untouched twenty provided the evidence of Kevin's awareness. Three beers later, Finn's twenty still had not moved. He sipped his beer and tried to understand why he was enjoying himself. He was jammed between two strangers, both of whom had their backs to Finn as they zeroed in on their female prey. The hoots from the college crowd were almost as annoying as the never-ending loud music – yet, for some reason he felt good. Maybe it was just the opportunity to get away from the office and forget about work for a few hours. Finn plopped the empty bottle on the bar next to his twenty. He knew he had to get back to work on his big case, but it was still refreshing to put aside Chelsea and Susan Garland – if only for one night.

Kevin appeared with another beer. "Good luck," he stated in bartender jargon indicating a buyback, despite the fact that Finn had yet to pay for any of the previous beers.

"Thanks, bartender." Finn deadpanned while raising his fresh beer in a salute.

The beer, the music, the loud voices – Finn was lost in the chaos, and he could not have been more content.

"Hey bartender!" Finn called. "Where's our hostess tonight?" Finn was feeling good and felt some facetime with Meg would only make him feel better.

Kevin passed by on his way to the other end of the bar. "She's off tonight." Making a second pass he provided additional details. "She's on a date."

Finn's upbeat spirits became like the air rushing out of a balloon. He was deflated. With his clientele currently satisfied Kevin stopped in front of Finn.

"What wrong with you?"

Finn looked away. "Nothing, go bartend."

The significance of Finn's sudden mood swing suddenly became clear to Kevin, and he ramped up to full ball breaking mode.

"Are we jealous? No, that's not possible. We don't give a shit about the girl, do we?"

Finn slowly turned, ready to explode.

"Finn? Finn Delaney?"

The voice interrupting Finn's imminent tirade came from his left, from the cop corner of the bar. Finn turned to face an advancing Biju Thomas. Finn extended his hand, but Biju bypassed the gesture and instead went in for a full hug.

"Finn Delaney – how the hell are you?"

"Great. How about you Sahib?" Finn responded using the good-natured nickname given to Biju in the police academy due to the fact he was the only recruit in the company of Indian descent.

The stranger on Finn's right had likely bagged his prey, evidenced by his quick exit accompanied by his female companion. The couple's departure left two vacant stools that were quickly occupied by Finn and Biju. Kevin plopped a Budweiser in front of Biju as Finn tapped his twenty-dollar bill, barroom etiquette indicating his desire to pay. Again, Kevin departed the area with the twenty undisturbed.

Finn and Biju had been classmates in the same police academy company. Since graduation, Biju had worked in the 105th precinct in eastern Queens. Biju droned on about life at the 105 then Finn had a turn to ramble on about Finn Delaney Investigations. The conversation then turned back to Biju.

"I'm getting married next year."

Finn raised his bottle. "Congratulations, Bro. Is it arranged?"

Biju laughed. "Get the hell out of here, man. This is the 21st century. I'm not agreeing to that arranged marriage shit." Biju sipped his beer before continuing. "Although to tell you the truth, there are some advantages to arranged marriages."

"Like what?" Finn questioned.

"The whole mindset, dude. Most of these arranged broads come to the table with a good attitude."

"What's that mean?"

Biju continued his explanation. "These arranged broads may be ugly as shit, but they don't expect too much – they don't break your balls. My fiancé is already breaking my balls to get a house we can't afford."

"What are you going to do?" Finn continued.

"I'm gonna do what every other American husband does – work as many jobs as I can to stop her from breaking my balls."

"How's the overtime in the 105?"

"Not good enough. I need a good, steady second front." Finn understood that Biju was using cop slang for an off-duty job.

"Any prospects?" Finn asked.

"Prospects?" Biju cupped his hands together. "I had it man, right here in the palms of my hands. The ultimate second front." Biju extended his arms to his sides. "And then it all fell apart."

"What happened?"

"My partner in the 105 was getting me into this sweet gig in Manhattan."

"What kind of gig?"

"He worked for these brothers who retired from the job – the Kelly's, I think. Anyway, these brothers have a security company that guards VIPs in some high scale hotel – some kind of visiting foreign royalty. The pay is over fifty dollars an hour and these Arab high rollers throw around hundreds in tips like its nothing."

Finn couldn't believe what he was hearing. Somehow, in the tranquility of his loud, tumultuous evening, the Garland case had been tossed back in front of him quicker then Kevin had tossed him beers. Whether he wanted to or not, Finn was now obligated to hear the rest of Biju's story.

"So, what happened to the gig?"

"Just as my partner is about to get me in, he ends up getting canned."

"What did he do?"

"I don't know. All I know is he got into a beef with some other cop who worked there – some douchebag detective from Intel."

"What's the detective's name?" Finn asked, his interest increasing.

"I don't know. Wait a minute – Delvecchio, I think. What difference does his name make?"

Finn took a big sip from his bottle and slammed the empty down hard on the bar. He leaned back on the stool and sighed. "Well, Sahib, let me tell you a little story."

DECEMBER 10th - Finn settled in on the stool, it's sliding legs creating the only sound to compete with Kevin's towel wiping orbit of the bar. He sipped the hot coffee and realized he was back in his element – the comfort zone of the empty bar. It had been five days since Biju Thomas had forced the Garland case back to the forefront of Finn's conscience. Now, he sat in his safe territory, enjoying a cup of Kevin' s fantastic coffee, awaiting the arrival of Biju and his partner, Vince Marino.

Finn also had not seen Meghan since Kevin's deflating revelation about her being on a date. Finn knew he was opening a door that would inevitably lead to non-stop ball breaking, but he didn't care.

"Hey Kev., you seen Meg lately?"

Kevin wasted no time in turning the screws. "You mean since she was out on a date last week?

"Yeah, you know what I mean. Just answer the question, please."

Kevin scratched his head. "Let's see, three days ago I saw her walking on Woodhaven holding hands with this real handsome guy, and I believe it was yesterday I think it was her I saw going into the Haven Motel with a different guy."

"Jerk!" Finn turned away from Kevin.

Kevin noticed the sullen look on Finn's face and experienced a rare moment of empathy. He leaned over the bar and addressed Finn quietly. "Hey, you know me. I'm just breaking your balls. As a matter of fact, I don't know where she was last week when she took off."

Finn did not turn and respond. His spirits were rising but he always had to wary of being set up for another zinger.

The light from the opening door momentarily broke the tranquil atmosphere of the dark, empty bar. Finn felt like he was at the fifty-yard line of a football field during the coin toss, with the ensuing introductions and handshakes of the four bar occupants. Ever the gracious host, Kevin provided a cup of his excellent coffee to Biju, and he seemed delighted when Vince spurned the coffee, and instead asked for a scotch on the rocks.

"My kind of guy," Kevin remarked as he put the glass down in front of Vince.

As the obligatory small talk commenced, Finn realized that Vince Marino was a caricature. He was one of those walking talking stereotypes that people from other parts of the country believe all New Yorkers look like and sound like. Vince appeared to be around 35-years-old, medium height, with an athletic build. His heavily pomaded black hair was the perfect complement to his spotless white track suit with both a Figaro chain and Italian horn hanging prominently around his neck. Finn also recognized the New York City stereotype in Vince's speech. He spoke quickly and succinctly in loud, expressive tones. He dropped his R's when they appeared before consonants, so when he asked Kevin for a glass of water, it came out "Lemme get a glass of watta." Vince also replaced the "th" at the beginning and end of words with a percussive "d" or "t" sound. His description of why he arrested someone for littering included, "Dat was tree times I told dat prick to pick dat shit up."

With the war stories concluded, Vince very eloquently told his tale of working for the Kelly brothers security company.

"Dat Delvecchio is a real scumbag."

Finn needed a little more detail, so he attempted to back Vince up a bit. “Vince, what exactly does the company do?”

“Dey protect dese Arabs – royal guys from some Arab country – some country dat begins wid a ‘B’ – Blame, Brine, something like dat.”

Kevin was not supposed to be a part of this conversation, but Finn realized that social graces were not his friend’s strong point as he inserted himself without invitation.

“Brains.” Kevin excitedly blurted as he leaned over the bar and smacked Finn’s shoulder. “Remember a while back we saw that news article about the king of brains.”

Vince was quick to substantiate. “Yeah, yeah – brains – I think dat’s it.”

Finn prayed that stupidity was not contagious. “I think we’re talking about the country of Bahrain.”

Vince and Kevin seemed unimpressed, based on the chorus of “whatever.”

Finn had an idea how to get Vince focused, and he was glad Kevin recognized his non-verbal cue and placed another scotch in front of Vince. The fresh drink seemed to have the desired effect in prompting Vince to continue his description of the security company.

“Dese brudders really stepped in shit. I heard dat when one of dem was working in the Intelligence Division, he did some work with dese Arabs and got in tight with dem. Dey set up da security company to protect dese guys and their families whenever dey come to dis country – which is all the time. The Arabs lease two floors of the Parkchester Hotel 365 days a year and da brudders got a piece of one of da floors set up as a command and control center – just like da one at 1PP – it's incredible. Whenever any of da Arabs is here, dey got the control center staffed and security in the areas where dey have da rooms."

Vince took a sip of scotch, giving Finn a chance to interject. "Sounds like a nice set up."

Vince put the empty glass on the bar. "You ain't kidding. 52-buck an hour to watch dese Arabs and dere wives and kids. But dat's not where da big money is."

Finn raised his eyebrows as Vince continued.

"Getting assigned to one dese Arabs is the big score. Once they're here, dey go all over da country. Let's say I get assigned to Prince Ali Baba, or whatever da hell their names are. If Ali Baba decides he's going to Las Vegas for a week, I gotta go with him. I never got one of dese details, but I heard da tips dese Arabs give at de end of the detail is insane."

Finn wanted to bring the story home. "So, what happened? Sounds like no one would leave this gig."

Vince sneered. "Dat asshole Delvecchio."

Finn nearly fell off the stool, but quickly recovered. "Who exactly is Delvecchio?"

"He's dis shithead detective from Intel. – thinks his shit don't stink."

"Why's that?"

"He's been up the brudders asses for years and he gets da prime friggin detail – the crown prince of dat Arab country."

"That's good?" Finn questioned

"Good?" Vince shot back "It's friggin great. Delvecchio plays nursemaid to dat Arab for a week or so and at the end of da trip, I heard dat prick gets tipped to the tune of around fifty grand."

"Fifty thousand dollars?" Finn's mouth was wide open.

" Dat's right bro. – fifty G's. Dat prick Delvecchio is totally in the pocket of dat Arab – probably blows him too." A sly smile emerged on Vince's face."Y'know what? For 50-K I'd probably blow him too."

Finn still didn't understand Vince's situation. "So what happened to you there?"

"Like I said, I never got da good details like dat prick Delvecchio. I would get assigned to the floor keeping watch over da rooms. Don't get me wrong. Any assignment paying 52-buck an hour was sweet."

Finn really wished Vince would get to the point, and he feared that the steady flow of scotch was only going to lengthen the tale.

"So why did you leave?"

"I'm getting to dat, bro. So, one night I'm assigned to da hall outside da rooms. There musta been fifty of dese Arabs and their families staying in da hotel. So, it's like midnight and I see dese two little kids running in the hall. Dese kids couldn't have been more den ten years old – two boys. I could give two shits dat they are raisin hell, but I see dem startin to mess with the fire alarm pull box. So, I go over to dem and I says to leave dat alone and go back to your room."

"That's it?" Finn responded

"No. Da kids start crying and run back into da room. A minute later dis crown prince asshole comes out and gets right in my face and starts screaming something about me never having the right to yell at his kids."

"What happened next?"

"I was seriously considering crowning dis prince asshole, when out from the room comes dis prick Delvecchio. Dis guy actually grabbed me by the collar and demanded that I apologize to this Arab. Can you believe dat?"

"Did you apologize?"

"Are you kiddin me bro. Even I have some friggin integrity. I pushed dat asshole off me and told him if he ever laid his hands on me again, I would kill him and his Arab boss."

"Wow!" Finn blurted

"Let's just say dat a few minutes after dis encounter, one of da brudders called me and wished me luck with my future endeavors" Vince laughed heartily before taking another sip of scotch.

Finn had just one more area to probe. "Do you know any other guys on the job who worked for that company?"

Vince shot Finn an incredulous look. "Tons of guys work for dem. Who wouldn't?"

"How about the guys in the inner circle – like Delvecchio?"

Vince stroked his chin and looked toward the Woodhaven Blvd. window. "Delvecchio was absolutely the main asshole, but dere were a couple of other guys giving him a run for his money."

"Who?"

"Some retired guy – a Pollock – I don't remember his name."

"Karpinski?"

"Yeah, yeah. Karpinski – Kowalsi. Some Polloack name like dat."

Anyone else?

"Dere was dis other asshole from IAB with a fancy haircut. He's a big asshole too."

Finn extended his hand to initiate a farewell handshake. "Thanks a lot, Vince. You've been a big help."

"No problem bro, and thanks for the booze."

A blast of bright light again disturbed the atmosphere. Biju was already out the door, but Vince stopped in the open doorway and called back to Finn. "You should really talk to my boy Petey Dwyer. He still works for da brudders and he's a real wash woman – he knows all the gossip. I'll give Petey a call."

One more expression of thanks was followed by a return to the dark tranquil environment.

ROAD RAGE

DECEMBER 15th - Finn peered out the window to the traffic flowing north and south on Woodhaven Blvd. There was something hypnotic about the post-rush hour flow of traffic – fast at first then stopping to regroup at the red traffic signal. It was much easier to get in touch with the boulevard from street level. Even though his office was just one short flight of stairs above ground level, that elevation resulted in an almost complete detachment from the rhythm of the street.

"Why don't you put that stupid sign in my window? You spend enough time here." Kevin slid a steaming cup of coffee in front of Finn and completed the preparation of his own cup with a bottle of Bailey's. "You should pay me. I'm a better secretary than that old bat you got stashed away across the street. I set up a place for your meetings, I feed you, I give you great advice."

Finn put his cup down on the bar. "Yeah, yeah – I get it. You're on one of nature's noblemen."

Kevin placed the Bailey's back in its designated spot on the shelf next to the cash register. He turned toward Finn and pointed both thumbs toward his own chest. "Just remember Fineous, the big guy here is always looking out for you."

Finn had at least a dozen smart ass answers at the ready, but his response was preempted by the sudden blast of light from the opening door. The intimate duo was now a trio with the entry of Pete Dwyer into the bar.

Pete looked all around while extending his hand to Finn. "Nice place. I'll have to check it out sometime at night. Are there a lot of broads here?"

Finn transitioned from a handshake to a shrug, but before he could state his uncertainty about the evening female situation, Kevin jumped right into the fray.

"Wall to wall women, my friend. You do need to check it out."

Finn shot Kevin a dual-purpose sneer – partly for inserting himself immediately into the conversation and partly because he had never seen a female population explosion inside the Shamrock.

Finn recognized immediately that Pete was no introvert, as he didn't hesitate to allow Finn time to offer coffee or another drink.

"How about a Bud, partner." Pete asked Kevin.

"You got it." Kevin placed the bottle on the bar – a bar devoid of any cash offerings. Obviously, Pete just assumed his drinks would be "on the arm" – well know cop jargon for free of charge.

Finn was always anxious in these situations. He knew it wasn't good to abruptly begin asking questions about the Kelly's security company right out of the box, but he was not skilled at insignificant social small talk. Pete lessened the tension when it quickly became apparent that Finn's actual dilemma might be how to shut him up.

Pete Dwyer seemed to be one of those guys who was comfortable talking at length about almost anything. Very quickly into the conversation, however, Finn understood exactly what Pete's favorite subject was – girls. Pete rambled on about old girlfriends, new girlfriends, girls he had sex with, and girls he was trying to have sex with. Finn raised his eyebrows when the subject briefly transitioned to Pete's wife and two daughters.

"A real family man," Finn thought. During Finn's brief NYPD career, he had seen a plethora of these wannabe Romeos – middle age guys with "perfect" family lives spending almost all their time on and off the job trying to score with girls. This cop characteristic seemed to be of such epidemic proportions that Finn wondered if being a snake was not an actual requirement listed on the police officer job description. At one point during this period of awareness, Finn began to question the integrity of his dad. Patrick Delaney had done nothing to merit any suspicion. By Finn's observations he had been an almost perfect father. But all these other cops trolling the city for girls were perfect family men too, weren't they? Finn actually considered asking his father about the subject, but he knew inside he could never really have that conversation with him. The subject became a dead issue. As far as he was concerned, his dad was of a rare breed. A cop who appeared to be a dedicated family man and who actually was a family man.

Pete finished his second beer and made the conversation transition incredibly easy for Finn. "So, Vince tells me you're looking to get some information about the Kelly's."

"Yeah, I want to know about the security company." Finn had a long story memorized about how he was considering trying to get a job there. Pete Dwyer spared him the charade and never gave him a chance to tell his story. Obviously, Pete didn't care one bit why he was asking about the company.

"I've worked for them for a couple of years. It's great money, but it's on and off work – nothing steady.

And when I get it, I only get assigned to the residence floor."

Finn feigned ignorance. "What other assignments are there?"

"Well, you can work in the command and control center, but there's nothing special about that assignment."

"Anything else?" Finn queried.

"The plum assignment is being assigned to specific VIPs when they're out of the hotel."

"What's that like?" Finn continued.

"You're their body guard whether they go across the street or across the country. Most of these assholes aren't very friendly, but the tips they give at the end of the assignment are crazy."

"How crazy?"

"Now I never actually got one of these details, but I talked to guys who got 5K like they were being given a five-dollar bill."

"Wow!" Finn tried to express real surprise.

"And that's not all. I heard one of the real inside guys who always gets the crown prince detail once got 50K." There was silence as Pete bit his lip and nodded his head before continuing. "That's why I'll never get the protection detail. This inside clique of guys has it all locked up." Pete put his empty bottle on the bar and shrugged. "Besides, I don't think I would want the detail now anyway."

Finn tipped his head to the side and slightly squinted. "Why not?"

"Too much shit going on."

"Like what?"

"I don't really know." Pete stated while accepting another fresh beer from Kevin. "But something happened - the past couple of months, everyone's been on edge."

Finn leaned back on the stool. "That's it?"

Pete glanced both ways and leaned forward, speaking in a tone noticeably lower than his previous volume. "I was working the resident floor one night a couple of months ago. It was real quiet on the floor because all the woman and kids were asleep, and the crown prince was out partying – that guy's a real snake."

Finn chuckled, but not because of the crown prince's description. It was amusing to hear someone like Pete Dwyer refer to someone else as a snake.

"So, the prince is out with his usual three stooges."

"Three stooges?" Finn no longer had to act confused.

"Yeah, the three guys who are always on his detail. Some guys from Intel. And IAB – I think one of them is retired by now. It's disgusting to see the way these guys fawn all over that prince. I wouldn't be surprised if they wipe his ass for him."

Finn nodded, trying to get the story moving again.

"So, I'm working the floor and sometime around two or three in the morning all hell breaks loose."

"What happened?"

"The whole entourage comes rushing onto the floor – the prince, his crew, the stooges – and everyone's screaming. The prince is screaming at his boys in Arabic. All of them are screaming at the stooges, and the stooges start screaming at me for some reason."

"What was going on?"

"I have no idea. But something really screwed up must have happened. Everyone – the prince, his boys, and the stooges were real scared about something."

"What did you do?"

"I told the stooges to back the "F" up. They're not gonna get all up in my face."

"Did you ever find out what happened?"

"No, but everything is still so tense there now. Even if I could get the detail, I wouldn't want it. Too much shit dealing with the stooges and their asshole prince."

Finn only had one more question.

"Who are the stooges?"

Pete was accommodating with information to the end.

"The main stooge is the guy from Intel. – Delvecchio. The guy from IAB is Defama, and the retired guy is a Pollock – I think his name is Karpinski. They were all nice enough guys, but since this shit happened, you can't even talk to them – turned out to be complete assholes."

As Pete was heading for the door he stopped and surveyed the empty bar one last time, nodding his head. "Yeah, if there's a lot of broads in this place I'm gonna have to check it out."

The door had closed behind Pete Dwyer, but Finn had yet to close the book on his information. He spun on the stool to face Kevin.

"When did they find that girl dead?"

"What girl?" Kevin stated while adding more Bailey's to his coffee.

"The girl - remember a while back you were talking about all the bad news in the paper, and you saw a story about a girl found dead in Manhattan."

Kevin sampled his newly energized coffee. "What dead girl in Manhattan? I slept with some girls from Manhattan who I thought were dead."

Finn's thumbs began working frantically on the screen of his iPhone. "Why I would even waste my time asking you for help is beyond me."

"I love you too." Kevin deadpanned.

Finn's thumbs stopped moving. "Here it is. Cynthia Dubois, 21, was found dead in a dumpster at 3 AM on the morning of October 2nd." Finn's breathing picked up in pace as he began manipulating his phone again.

"What are you doing now? Checking on the king of brains schedule." Kevin chuckled as he started wiping down the bar.

Finn completely ignored the snide remark and continued his check. "I have to look at my notes to see when Chelsea Garland went missing. Here it is. She was last seen on the evening of October 1st in Manhattan." Finn stared out to Woodhaven Blvd. speaking in a very low tone meant only for his own benefit." Chelsea goes missing on the night of October 1stt and they find Cynthia Dubois in a dumpster the next morning."

Finn kept staring out the window while tapping the fingers of his right hand on the bar. He bit his lip as his tapping became stronger. Finally, his right hand pounded the bar, bringing Kevin running from the opposite side of the bar.

"What the hell are you doing?"

"Why didn't I ask him?" Finn shrieked.

"Ask him what?"

Before Finn could respond, the blast of light signaled an entry into the Shamrock. Finn turned toward the door, and his eyes widened.

"Some double-parked asshole has me boxed in. Any idea where the shithead might be?"

"Try the Spanish chicken joint across the street." Armed with Kevin's lead, Pete Dwyer began an about face, but Finn wasn't about to let him get away again.

"Hey Pete. Can I ask you one more question?"

Pete stepped away from the door. "Sure."

"Do you remember the exact date all that shit took place with the stooges and the prince?"

"No." Pete's response completely deflated Finn. Pete reached into his back pocket, pulling out a small notebook. "It shouldn't be too hard to figure out though. I always keep track of the days I work there in this notebook. The first couple of months I got shortchanged hours – so never again. Every hour I work goes right into the book."

Finn instantly perked up as Pete turned pages.

"Let's see…I worked a few day shifts during September….hmm – this is it. I worked 6 PM to 6 AM October 1st into October 2nd."

Finn could hardly restrain his excitement. "Thanks…thanks a lot Pete – and oh yeah – check the chicken place."

Once they were alone again, Finn jumped off the stool, his weak right knee slightly buckling from the sudden impact. He paced back and forth, working the discomfort out of the knee. "What do you think of that?" He bellowed.

"Think of what?" Kevin responded.

Finn stopped pacing. "You can't be that stupid, can you?"

Kevin shrugged and smiled. "Maybe."

"Look Einstein, Chelsea Garland is last seen in Manhattan on October 1st. Cynthia Dubois is found in a dumpster early the next morning. That same night and early morning, something big happens that scares the shit out of the crown prince and his security detail."

"That don't prove a thing!" Kevin stated defiantly while cleaning beer mugs.

"It doesn't? How about the fact that Delvecchio, the detective from the Intelligence Division has been constantly visiting Susan Garland to see if she has heard from Chelsea. And how about the fact that Delvecchio and his cronies were with the prince on the same night Cynthia Dubois is killed and Chelsea goes missing, and there're all scared shitless about something. And how about Delvecchio walking into the 7th Precinct with Cynthia Dubois' killer - Come on"

"Well, maybe you do have something, but what are you going to do about it?"

"I need to go see Susan Garland – now!"

When he arrived in Broad Channel, Finn's senses were more aware of what was going on around him then they had been previously. As he paced through the swirling December wind, dirt, paper, and even some remnants of Autumn leaves danced in the breeze in little groups on the sidewalk, Finn was relieved to observe no evidence of Delvecchio or anyone else watching or following him. He was disappointed, however, to see no sign of the homeless lady who seemed to be a fixture on Cross bay Blvd. during every visit to Susan's. He wanted to talk to this lady and gain some insights into the pie eating song.

The setting was the same – the players seated at the large mahogany table in the dimly lit living room. The script, however, was completely different. Finn was tempted to describe Susan Garlands's demeanor as bubbly. Was this complete shift in attitude the result of the cryptic pie eating message from the weird homeless woman? How could that be?

Whatever the reason, Finn was glad to be dealing with the perky, upbeat Susan, as opposed to the morose, sullen woman he had come to know.

"I wanted to update you about some new information, Susan." Finn accessed the notes screen on his iPhone. He informed Susan of the timeline regarding the murder of Cynthia Dubois and the last time Chelsea was seen. He also told her of the commotion in the hotel with Delvecchio and the crown prince at the same time. Finn put his phone back in his pocket. "Susan, I don't want you to talk to Delvecchio or anyone from the police. There's something very weird going on here with the police and I don't want you to talk to them until I figure this out."

Susan's smile was indicative of her continuing attitude. "Oh, don't worry about that Finn. I stopped talking to Delvecchio and his friends the moment you gave me that message from Chelsea."

Finn was still a bit confused by the message. "Run that by me again, Susan. How are you sure that was a message from Chelsea? It sounded to me more like the ranting of a crazy bag lady."

Susan reached across the table and placed her hand on top of Finn's. "I haven't decided if you're a good private investigator, but I have decided that I trust you, and that's all that's important."

Finn slightly smiled while trying to determine if the comment was a complement or an insult.

"Like I told you, that message was a made-up song Chelsea used to sing. It was such a running joke for us because I got the words wrong. She was singing blindfolded but I thought she was singing blind or dead. I am one hundred percent sure that this was Chelsea's way of getting a message to me that she is ok."

Finn leaned back from the massive table. "I don't want to dampen your spirits, Susan, but why didn't she just call you on the phone?"

The look on Susan's face gave Finn cause to believe that she had just found the answer regarding his competency as an investigator. "Look, you have to understand that Chelsea is an extremely bright girl." She leaned forward and put her hand back on Finn's. "I know every mother thinks their child is the greatest, but this is different. Chelsea is extremely smart, both academically and with situational awareness of what is going on around her."

Finn shook his head slightly. "I don't think I see your point, Susan."

"The point is that something happened that night – something big, and whatever it was, Chelsea instantly recognized that she was in danger, and that the danger she faced was from the police."

Finn remained silent, mouth open as he tried to formulate a question. After a brief moment to allow Finn an opening to jump in, Susan continued,

"Don't you see, Finn. For some reason Chelsea determined that the police are a threat to her. She can't use her phone, and she probably got rid it so she could not be tracked. She can't use a credit card or a Metro Card either. That's why she withdrew the maximum of a thousand dollars from the ATM." Susan waved her right hand in a dismissive gesture. "I don't know exactly how this homeless lady you talk about figures into all this, but obviously, Chelsea has decided to trust you too, and she used you to carry her message to me."

Finn still had nothing to say, so Susan continued.

"Why do you think Delvecchio has been constantly calling me? He's scared. Chelsea knows something that is scaring the hell out of him and he's going to do anything to find her."

Finn shrugged as he assumed the role of the depressed party at the table. "Susan, I really don't know what I can do now."

"You don't have to do anything, Finn."

"What?"

"Chelsea reached out to you once and she'll do it again." This time both of Susan's hands covered Finn's hands. "When she does, it will be up to you to get her to safety."

Finn had completely lost his sense of awareness as he pressed on the key fob to unlock the doors of the Toyota. He smiled as he slid into the driver's seat. So many thoughts had been rushing through his head during the short walk to his car, he only now realized that an army of Delvecchios and bag ladies could have set upon him from all sides and he would have been oblivious to them.

He still had no idea what to do next, except to follow Susan's advice and wait for Chelsea to reach out to him. Finn eased out into the right lane on Cross bay and immediately found himself stopped for the red light at the next intersection. The light turned green, but nothing happened. Finn was second in line behind a white Mercedes E300 and the vehicle hadn't moved. Finn was never a stressed-out candidate for road rage, but even his patience had limits. After at least ten seconds of no movement, Finn tapped his horn.

It happened so fast. Most of these road rage incidents escalate very quickly. Finn didn't consciously recall getting out of the car, it was likely some macho reflex imbedded in even the most rational thinking men. His remaining memories were like a series of snapshots in an album. There was the punch landing on his jaw followed by the pain erupting from the point of impact. There was the crimson leaking from both his nostrils after the second blow. There was also the image of a fist plowing into his stomach. The final image was the most enduring. He lay on his back on the boulevard, his chest gently rising and sinking with each shallow breath he drew in. Two images above him came into semi-focus. The same two young well-dressed Middle Eastern males who had come out of the Mercedes. The stockier male squatted next to Finn and pinched his cheeks between the fingers of his right hand.

"You need to learn some manners, friend."

As the male began to rise from his squat, he made a parting statement.

"And keep your nose out of what doesn't concern you. You've been warned!"

Finn remained recumbent as he tried to collect all his senses. Thankfully, his Toyota shielded him from traffic. Even so, he was still visible to passing traffic in the adjoining lanes, but no one stopped to assist. Finn had no expectation of help, however – this was New York City.

Finn closed his eyes to continue his physical recovery. His quick assessment revealed that he could feel everything, and all his parts seemed to be moving properly. The pain in his face and stomach was also receding. He took a deep breath and tensed his body for the return to an upright position. He opened his eyes and let out a shriek. Hovering over him was the homeless bag lady, and she appeared to be in the process of going through his pockets.

Finn shot to his feet so quickly that he almost staggered into the adjacent lane of traffic as he battled lightheadedness. "Stay away from me you demented bitch!" Finn cautiously stepped backwards, feeling for his car door, maintaining surveillance on the woman.

"Go to her!" the bag lady growled.

Finn laid on the horn again until the homeless woman shuffled away from the front of the Toyota. His body and ego were bruised, but both would heal. The most troubling aspect of the fiasco had been the Middle Eastern man's warning. What the hell was going on with this case?

Finn was elated that no one was home, so he did not have to go through a scene explaining his new bruises. He went directly to his room and locked the door behind him. Finn reached behind his closet door mirror and removed a piece of paper that had been taped to the rear side of the mirror. He sat on the edge of the bed with the paper in his left hand. With his right hand he entered the numbers into the dial in the proper sequence. Finn pulled down on the handle and the safe door opened. He reached into the darkness of the safe's interior and retrieved one item. Finn never did have a fondness for firearms, but with his status as a medically retired police officer, he was able to obtain a full carry handgun license. Finn wasn't interested in carrying a firearm, but at his father's insistence he purchased a compact gun – a 9MM semi-automatic Smith & Wesson M&P Shield – a gun that he locked away in his safe, with no intention of ever carrying. Finn pulled the Velcro tight around his left ankle. The Shield was going to be a fixture there from now on.

Finn took off his jacket as his thoughts shifted to the crazy lady. "Go to her" – what the hell did that mean. Just then, a new warning alarm activated in Finn's brain. His jacket – that crazy bitch was going through his pockets. Finn grabbed the jacket off the bed and inspected the pockets. He only had some loose change and a few dollar bills inside, and they all seemed to be accounted for. But what was the crumbled piece of paper in with the money? That wasn't his, was it? Finn uncrumpled the paper and read its contents out loud. "190 Morgan Avenue."

He stared at his image in the closet mirror. "I don't know anyone at this address, do I?" The crazy lady echoed in his head "Go to her." Finn scratched his head and continued to address himself in the mirror. "Is this what I was waiting for? Is she reaching out to me?"

NEWTOWN CREEK

CHRISTMAS EVE – Finn was in the midst of a self-imposed nine day holding pattern. The shots he took on Cross Bay Blvd. had shaken him, and he quickly decided it was time for the boss of Finbar Delaney Investigations Inc. to take vacation over the holiday season. Maybe his mind would clear when the new year arrived, and the correct path forward would be obvious. Right now, however he was conflicted. Finn had become personally invested in the Garland case, and he sincerely wanted to do everything he could to help Susan. On the other hand, there were a lot of very weird circumstances arising in this case and he had no desire to have the next reservation inside a dumpster. Normally, he would go directly to his father for counsel, but in this case, he couldn't. He was relieved when Patrick apparently bought the story of a quick turn into an open bathroom medicine cabinet mirror as the cause of his facial bruises. If Finn told his dad about the assault on him, Patrick would immediately shut the case down. Even that prospect had Finn confused. What if Chelsea was alive somewhere? Would exposing Delvecchio help her or hurt her? He didn't know. Finn had been thinking on this subject for nine days and had yet to reach a conclusion.

Presently, his biggest decision was whether he should launch a frontal assault or attack from the right flank. Finn abruptly shut off his Xbox. He could not even focus on a late morning Christmas Eve Call of Duty battle. He needed an environment where he could think.

"Ho, Ho, Ho, - Merry Christmas. I didn't expect to see you here today. I thought Super-Sleuth Incorporated was on vacation." Kevin wiped down the bar with a towel. The pub had only been officially open for fifteen minutes, but the two residents of stools appeared completely inebriated.

Finn settled in on a stool. His attention was drawn to the ridiculous-looking Santa Claus hat Kevin was wearing. The hat had blinking, multi-colored lights, and what appeared to be grass sticking out of the top.

"What's up with that monstrosity?" Finn pointed to the headpiece.

"Just staying in the spirit of the holiday season, my friend."

Finn continued pointing. "Why is there grass growing out of your head?"

"Grass? Haven't you ever seen mistletoe?"

"Yeah," Finn snickered. "I have seen mistletoe. That's why I asked why you had grass growing out of your head."

"Sometimes, one must improvise." Kevin winked. "Don't worry, the ladies will understand what they are standing under."

"Lucky them," Finn chuckled

Kevin placed a hot cup of coffee in front of Finn and held up the Bailey's. "Come on – not even for Christmas?"

"Nope," Finn said while enjoying the first sip. "This is all I need."

"Suit yourself," Kevin responded while spiking his cup with a holiday portion of Bailey's.

Finn placed the cup on the bar. "Where's our hostess? Is she working later today?"

Kevin's cup joined Finn's on the bar. "You know something, Finbar," Kevin was not smiling. "I break your balls a lot, but I've been meaning to tell you something for a long time."

"What?"

"What you did to Meghan sucked!"

Finn made a move off the stool and Kevin reacted. "Go ahead! Run away like you did before." Finn resettled on the stool and Kevin continued. "Once you hooked up with Jen you treated that poor girl like she had a contagious disease."

"You knew the deal," Finn responded weakly. "Jen had a problem with me talking to other girls."

Kevin pounded his fist on the bar. "This wasn't another girl! This was Meg – our friend since the first grade. I always knew that bitch Jen was all wrong for you, but you never asked me for my opinion."

"Well, thanks Dr. Phil," Finn commented very sarcastically.

Kevin was still rolling. "If you treated me like that I would tell you to go screw yourself, but for some reason, this girl still likes you."

"What are you talking about?"

Kevin's voice was rising with his frustration level. "Are you blind? You can't see that Meg still likes you? And I stand behind this bar every day and watch you continue to treat her like crap."

Finn stared into his coffee cup while Kevin moved to the end of the bar to tend to the needs of one of the drunks.

A much more mellow bartender returned to Finn's position. "So, have you fully recovered from your beating?

"Very funny." Finn welcomed the verbal shot. At least it moved the conversation away from Meghan.

"So, what are you gonna do with the big case?" Kevin inquired.

Finn shook his head and looked down. "I don't know. Maybe there's nothing to any of this."

"Nothing?" Kevin shot back. "What about all this great evidence you told me about.? What about all the stuff with the detective from the Intelligence Division and how he seems to be turning up everywhere – the mother's house – the three-name killer – the Arab security company?

Finn continued to look down. "Who knows? It may all be a big coincidence."

"Coincidence?" Kevin laughed. "Was your beating a coincidence?"

Finn looked up at Kevin. "Maybe – or maybe it was what it appeared to be – a stupid road rage incident."

Kevin continued, "And the crazy bag lady who sings to you and gives you addresses?"

Finn shrugged. "She might be just what she appears to be – nuts!"

"And the address?" Kevin questioned.

"Who knows?" Finn repeated the shrug. "Maybe it's a homeless colony. I don't know anymore."

Kevin moved to the other end of the bar to service the second drunk. "You know, Finbar, you may be on to something. Don't get yourself wrapped up in all this crap that may turn out to be nothing anyway."

Kevin pushed a newspaper in front of Finn. "Here's the Post. I have to go downstairs for a few. Jimmy's here early today and I have to show him a few things in the office. Call me if anyone comes in."

"What's up Jimmy?" Finn said.

Jimmy Costigan had just entered the pub. He waved to Finn as he followed Kevin down the stairs. Jimmy was the regular nighttime bartender at the Shamrock, and for years, Finn blamed Kevin for the embarrassment of getting Jimmy's name wrong. Since Kevin was the regular bartender on the day shift, barroom jargon caused some regulars to refer to him as Kevin – Day and Jimmy Costigan as Jimmy – Night. When first introduced to Jimmy Costigan, Finn was painfully ignorant of barroom jargon, so when Kevin introduced him as Jimmy – Night, Finn thought his name was James Knight. Finn's error was discovered in a most embarrassing manner. Finn possessed above average computer design skills, so when Kevin asked him to design the invitations to Jimmy's wedding, Finn happily agreed. People still talked about receiving an invitation to the wedding of Marie Molina and James Knight.

Finn paged through the paper while finishing up his coffee. Ten minutes later Kevin returned behind the bar. "Anything new in the paper?" Kevin asked

"The Giants suck!" Finn responded.

"That's new?" Kevin fired back. They both shared a laugh. Kevin went back to wiping down the bar while Finn retuned to the paper. The bar towel came gliding to a stop in front of the newspaper."

"Hey Finn, where was the address that homeless broad gave you?"

Finn did not look up from the paper. "Williamsburg – Brooklyn – 190 Morgan Avenue."

"What is it?"

Finn looked up at Kevin. "I googled it. It's some kind of factory right on the water."

"What water?"

"Newtown Creek?"

"What Creek?"

"Forget it," Finn snickered. "I wouldn't expect you to be able to get much further than the Atlantic Ocean."

"Real funny! Anyway, you're probably right. The crazy broad probably dropped that paper in your pocket accidentally while she was trying to get your money – probably nothing to that address."

Kevin continued wiping the bar and Finn dove back into the newspaper. A couple entered for an early holiday drink, and the jolly bartender with the flashing Santa hat with grass growing out of his head happily served them. Once the couple were properly imbibing, Kevin drifted back to Finn.

"I just have one more question." Kevin began.

"Yes." The remark brought Finn's head out of the newspaper again.

"As remote as the possibility may be, what if that girl is waiting for help at 190 Morgan Avenue?"

Finn did not respond as Kevin slid his towel down the bar. Finn looked out the window for several minutes. He visited the men's room and returned to the same position of deep thought. Finally, he took a deep breath and rubbed his hands together. "Hey Kev., do you still have your ID card from my company?"

"Of course. Why wouldn't I?"

Finn moved right on to his second question. “Do you think Jimmy could cover for you?”

“Maybe, why?”

“I need for you to come with me somewhere.”

“Where?”

“190 Morgan Avenue.”

Finn and Kevin stared at each other for several seconds. Kevin broke the trance when he stepped back, turned to the left and called out, “Jimmy!”

As the Toyota pulled into Woodhaven Blvd., Kevin rubbed his hands together. “OK, boss, tell me what we’re getting into.”

Finn handed Kevin his iPhone. “Pull up the address on Google and you can take a look.”

Kevin began manipulating the phone while Finn explained what he already knew. “I really don’t have a clear idea of what we’re getting into. As far as I can tell, 190 Morgan Avenue is some type of waterfront warehouse in the East Williamsburg section of Brooklyn. The warehouse is large ab appears to be recessed back from Morgan Avenue and borders Newtown Creek.”

“Again, with this Newtown Creek. I’ve lived here all my life and I never heard of it.”

“No offense,” Finn responded, but I’m pretty sure there are many things you are not aware of.”

“Just keep driving, boss,” Kevin said.

“Anyway, Newtown Creek is one of New York City’s lesser known navigable waterways.”

“What’s that mean?” Kevin asked

"Navigable means that boats are able to navigate to open waters. The creek leads out to the East River and New York Harbor."

Kevin had accessed the Street View of the address. "Hey, the warehouse is one of those Chinamen places. I can see Chinese writing all over the walls."

"That's correct," Finn responded. "I believe the warehouse is the home of Sun-Yen Imports. I don't know much else about the area."

Finn knew very little about this section of Brooklyn, other than it had transitioned at some point in recent history from a dreary industrial zone into the Mecca of the hipster culture in New York City. Trendy cafes, bars, and galleries shared the real estate with run down factories and warehouses. He read in his online research that rezoning in the area during the 1990s was the dramatic factor in the gentrification of the area, characterized by hipster culture, an art scene, and vibrant nightlife. During the early 2000s the neighborhood became a center for indie rock and electroclash, and had been nicknamed "Little Berlin."

When Finn turned left from Grand Avenue onto Morgan Avenue, traffic was relatively light. So light that if Finn or Kevin had been paying any attention to their surroundings, they would have noticed the two dark sedans with tinted windows that had been pacing them since Woodhaven Blvd.

Finn pulled to the curb outside the long gravel driveway that led to the warehouse. Off in the distance, some workers were visible scurrying around a truck parked in a loading dock bay. Kevin took in the scene from the passenger seat and then turned to face Finn. "Now what, Sherlock?"

"I guess I'll take a look around." Finn did not sound very confident. "You stay with the car."

"Sure thing, boss." Kevin saluted.

Finn walked down the long driveway and stood outside the truck bays with his hands on his hips. What was he doing standing among all these scurrying Asian truck drivers and factory workers? He looked down and started shuffling his feet in the gravel while considering that maybe has was right all along. The information he was depending on was just the rantings of a crazy bag lady. With one last kick of gravel he turned to be begin his retreat back to Morgan Avenue. As he turned, he saw it. Funny, it had been there all along, but this was the first time his brain processed its presence. Instead of walking toward the street, he chose the opposite route toward the water.

It was a large vessel. Finn estimated that the boat was about 150-feet long and had four levels. It looked like a ferry or one of those sight-seeing boats, but it was also obvious that the boat had been docked for many years. All the visible wood planking was worn or rotting with peeling paint everywhere. Through the peeling paint on the planks of the starboard bow "SEA BUDDY" was visible

Finn stood at the edge of the dock, staring at the dilapidated water craft. Now what? He now had an old, run down boat to complement his Asian import workers, but it still gave him no clue as to why he was at this location. Maybe there was nothing strange going on, other than his own paranoia. Maybe Susan Garland didn't have a storybook relationship with her daughter, and maybe Chelsea's going away letter was real. Maybe the cryptic pie message was nothing more than the incoherent ramblings of a bag lady, and that Susan's response was a desperate mother looking for a sign – any sign to grab onto. Maybe his fisticuffs on Cross bay Blvd. had been what it appeared to be – a road rage incident, and that the warning from his adversary had simply been a caution not to honk his horn again. And maybe the murder of poor Cynthia Dubois had absolutely nothing to do with his case. Finn scooped up a handful of gravel and tossed it into the polluted waters of Newtown Creek.

"It's about time you got here!"

Finn spun to his left. The woman was dressed like any other urban New Yorker. She was casual, but smartly dressed in jeans, a hipster jacket, and a neck scarf. Her face was made up, and not over done and her long black hair was pulled back into a pony-tail. Finn took her in. She was actually quite pretty, but her beauty was not Finn's focus. There was something very familiar about this attractive twenty-something girl, but Finn was having no success determining where the familiarity may lie.

"You wanna give me a hand with this, sport?"

The girl was struggling with a large wooden plank that appeared to be about eight feet long and a foot wide. Finn grabbed one side of the plank as the girl continued the instructions.

"Put it over the bow."

"Good lad." She congratulated Finn with a slap on the back as she tested the plank with her right foot.

"Follow me sport," the girl instructed as she began her journey across the newly created bridge to the boat.

"Is this safe?" Finn called out.

The girl hopped down to the deck. "I guess you'll find out laddy."

Finn decided his best course of action was to look straight ahead, and six quick but careful steps later he joined the girl on the deck of the Sea Buddy.

"Pull the plank to the deck." Finn obeyed and then watched the girl disappear through a door near the stern. An instant later her head reappeared. "Well, Come on!"

A ladder to the next deck and a walk down a long, dark narrow passageway left Finn standing next to the girl in front of a discolored, peeling door. The girl rapped three times on the door. "I'm home and I've brought a guest for dinner."

The door opened, and the girl entered the cabin. Finn hesitated until the girl beckoned. "Come on in. I know you hardly know us but you're going to have to share a mattress with one of us."

Finn could hardly find a place on the floor to stand as just about the entire area of the tiny cabin floor was covered by two mattresses. The girl with the pony-tail plopped on the vacant mattress leaving Finn's eyes to adjust to the inadequate illumination being supplied by one small lamp. On the mattress adjacent to the pony-tail girl sat another figure. As this new figure came into better focus, Finn again had the feeling that he knew this person. This time, however, there was no mystery in the familiarity. Sitting on the mattress four feet from him was Chelsea Garland. Like the Sea Buddy, Finn was looking at a worn out, weathered version of something that was once the picture of grace. Even in this deteriorated condition, there was no mistaking the girl on the mattress as the same girl in those professional looking photos on the Garland's living room wall.

There was so much to say and so much ground to cover, but Finn decided to begin with the basics. "Hi Chelsea."

"Hello." Chelsea waved her arm toward the bottom of her mattress. "Sit, please."

Finn had to make several maneuvers to get comfortable. His right knee injury made it very difficult to sit in a cross-legged position. Chelsea seemed to perceive that Finn had finally attained a somewhat bearable position.

"What's your name?"

"Finn….Finn Delaney."

"I see you know who I am Mr. Delaney. I brought you here because I have no choice but to trust you."

"That's very complementary, Chelsea, but why the hell would you trust me?"

Chelsea Garland nodded toward the other mattress. "Because my friend says I should trust you."

Finn stared thoughtfully at the pony-tail girl while Chelsea continued. "You've already met, but I guess you still need a formal introduction."

Finn looked back at Chelsea. "The first time I met your friend was out on the dock, but…," Finn stopped abruptly in mid-sentence, his mouth wide open. His eyes joined his mouth in a wide-open state as he turned and pointed at the pony-tail girl. Awareness had suddenly set in. "You're her! You're the demented bag lady."

The pony-tail girl laughed. "What a great introduction. It's a pleasure to meet you too Mr. Delaney."

Finn looked back to Chelsea. He did not say a word, but then again, he didn't have to. Chelsea took a deep breath. "Well, I guess I better start at the beginning." She adjusted herself in her corner of the mattress before continuing. "On that last night – I don't remember the date – it's all a blur now. Anyway, this girl on my job invited me to go out with her after work. We were supposed to go to The Carleton Club, this real upscale club down the block from my job. Well, Linda and I no sooner get into the club when she gets a call from home. Her grandmother slipped and fell in their house and had to go to the hospital. Linda had to run out of there and now I'm alone. I didn't want to go home, so I decided to stay in the club for a while. I realized I was going to have to go home alone at some point, so I'm sitting at the bar, enjoying the music and sipping club sodas. I was probably at the bar for about an hour when I noticed some excitement or commotion on the other side of the bar. It looked like some type of entourage was passing through the floor and I figured that some VIP or celebrity must have entered the club. I only saw him for an instant, but it looked like the center of attention was a very distinguished looking, handsome, Middle Eastern guy. I knew he was the focal point because he seemed to have an army of security around him. The entourage drifted away, I assumed to a private part of the club, and everything became relatively quiet again. About an hour later I put down my last club soda and was getting ready to make my exit. Before I can get up from my stool this guy approaches and introduces himself. My initial reaction was that he was a good-looking guy, but much too old for me – probably in his late forties. Anyway, this guy introduces himself as an NYPD detective and shows me a gold police badge. He said that he was the security for the crown prince of some country – I don't remember which one – and that the prince was having a private party in a VIP section of the club. The detective told me that the prince had seen me as he passed through the bar, and that he would like such a pretty lady to attend his party. I know it was stupid to get involved with this, but what girl wouldn't be flattered with an invitation from a prince. And I thought I'd be safe – how could I be safer then with an NYPD escort. So, I follow the detective up a set of stairs and down a long hall. The detective knocks on a door and while we are waiting, I can hear shouting from the other side of the door – and it didn't sound like happy, partying shouting. So, the door opens and there's this other middle age guy who looks like a cop standing there with the most frightened look I have ever seen on a person. He looks right at my escort and says 'Del – we got a big problem! He fuckin killed her, man!' They both run inside the room and I'm just standing just outside the door – paralyzed. In a split second I'm taking in everything going on inside the room. A lot of Middle Eastern and white guys are all yelling at each other. In the middle of the floor is that handsome prince guy, and he's waving his arms yelling at everyone. I see something on the floor in front of the prince, and for a moment, I'm not sure what it is. Then, I realize – it's a blond girl, and she's not moving. I was beginning to panic, and I still had not moved. I heard the prince yelling something about no female can ever laugh at him or disrespect him. I then saw one of the other Middle Eastern guys grab my escort by the shirt collar and yell in his face, 'No one can ever tell this story – do you understand?' Right at that point I began to realize the gravity of my situation and I started backing quietly down the hall. After a few back steps I turned and ran for the stairway. Just as I hit the stairway door I could hear shouts from the other end of the hall saying, 'that girl – don't let her get away.'"

Finn finally decided to break into the story. "How did you get away – they were so close to you?"

Chelsea smiled. "I went up the stairs and just sat on the next landing. I knew I couldn't outrun them, so I gambled that they would not even consider that I would run upstairs to a dead end."

Finn nodded. "Smart."

"Well, thank you, Mr. Delaney. With your blessing I will continue."

"By all means." Finn stated.

"I stayed on that landing for about a half hour. I figured I had waited long enough so I blessed myself and tried to look as casual as possible as I walked down the stairs to the first floor, across the club floor and out to the street. I went into the avenue and started looking for a cab, but reality hit me. I had just witnessed something really bad – probably a murder – and now NYPD detectives were after me so that the story would never be told. I was in big trouble and I couldn't go home. I knew there were all kinds of ways that the cops could track me, so I knew I had to act fast. I went to the Bank of America ATM and withdrew the thousand-dollar cash maximum. I left my smartphone at the ATM so I couldn't be tracked with it, and I had no use for my credit cards, which could also provide my location. So, I had a thousand dollars in my pocket and I was alone on the Eastside of Manhattan in the middle of the night, trying to figure out somewhere safe to go."

"So how did you end up here?" Finn interjected.

Chelsea glanced over to the other mattress and smiled. "Tiffany really saved my ass – at least up to now."

The pony-tail girl leaned forward on her hands and knees, then lifted her right hand and extended it toward Finn. "Tiffany Lawrence – artist, painter, actor – at your service."

Tiffany retreated from the handshake to her previous position on the mattress as Chelsea continued.

"A couple of months ago, some of my friends were looking for somewhere new to go to on a weekend night and someone suggested we check out Williamsburg and all the hipster places. So, on a Saturday night we end up at this place across the street – The Bookcase – you probably saw it while you were out on the street."

Finn shrugged his shoulders.

"Anyway, I'm in the bar and almost immediately this creep begins coming on to me, and he won't take a hint that I'm not interested. He keeps following me everywhere I go, and my friends are no help at all. I'm really beginning to get nervous when out of the blue Tiffany appears and tells the creep that if he doesn't disappear immediately she's going to cut his nuts off."

Chelsea and Tiffany glanced at each other and laughed.

Finn wasn't sure what the laugh meant. "So, what happened?"

"He disappeared, and I had a new hero. She was such a nice person, we really hit it off. And then when she told me she lived on a boat, and that it was right across the street – well, I just had to see this boat parked in the middle of Brooklyn." Chelsea sighed deeply and looked again toward Tiffany. "In that moment when I needed someplace safe to go, Tiffany's boat was the only place I could think of." Chelsea pointed to the other mattress again. "Tiffany can tell you all about this boat."

"Of course, I'll explain to Mr. Delaney." Finn flashed back to her introduction as an actor. Tiffany certainly had that over the top, Shakespearean tone whenever she spoke.

"I moved here from Ohio three years ago to find fame and fortune, and so far, all I found is this boat." Finn perceived the pause to be the actor in Tiffany giving her audience time to respond with laughter.

"In the great New York City tradition of squatting, some fellow artists I met directed me to the boat as a place where I could set up residence. I now know almost everything there is to know about the Sea Buddy. Some of my neighbors rigged up electricity and a makeshift plumbing system in this four-floor, 145-foot long fine vessel. We have some crazy parties here that go on all night long."

Finn was more interested in the boat's history then its party potential.

"How did it get here?"

"The Sea Buddy was a 650-passenger ferry built in 1978. By 2008 it was no longer being used as a ferry and the owner converted it to living space and rented out rooms. The artsy crowd, which is still here, could use any of three small motorboats to make the trip to Manhattan in ten minutes. The boats are still tied up outside, but I don't know if anyone uses them anymore. After all, the artsy scene here in Williamsburg is just as good, if not better than the scene in Manhattan.

"So, you pay rent for this room?" Finn questioned.

Tiffany put up her right hand in the universal signal for stop.

"Let me finish, Mr. Delaney. I was told that after Superstorm Sandy hit in 2012, the owner just abandoned the boat, resulting in an instant squatter's paradise."

Tiffany extended her arms. "So, Mr. Delaney, how do you like my humble abode?"

"It's great!" Finn fabricated from his position in this eight- foot by eight- foot cabin. There was still much more he desired to know.

"What about the whole bag lady routine. How did that work?"

Chelsea continued the narrative. "Once I got here, I felt safe. I had a thousand dollars, so with Tiffany shopping I could sustain myself on board while I figured out some way to see what was going on in the outside world. I desperately wanted to get word to my mom – she must be going crazy – but I couldn't risk it. I knew that these cops who were after me would be all over her looking for signs of where I was."

Chelsea bowed her head respectfully and extended her arm toward Tiffany. "It was my actor-friend who came up with the bag lady idea. She figured that by hanging out in an area where she could see my house she could get an idea of what was going on. And it worked. Once she saw the cops get in your face we figured we could trust you."

"Thanks." Finn stated.

"Don't flatter yourself," Chelsea responded. "We were looking for anyone to reach out to and you were the only rube who fit the bill."

Chelsea leaned forward and touched Finn's knee. "By the way, how is my mother?"

"Much better, since I delivered the pie message."

Chelsea leaned back, clapped her hands and shrieked, "I knew she's understand!"

"Well, that's pretty weird if you ask me." Finn said.

"Actually," Chelsea shot back, "I don't recall anybody asking you, but you have to admit it worked, didn't it?"

Tiffany took the lead again. "Then when you took that beating from those two guys, I figured you had to be ok. So, I stuck this address in your jacket pocket. And here you are."

Chelsea leaned forward again. "By the way, who exactly are you, Mr. Delaney? Please tell me you're not my mom's new boyfriend?"

Chelsea and Tiffany shared another laugh. Finn didn't really see the hilarity of the comment, but he proceeded with his role. "I'm a private investigator hired by your mother."

"Excellent!" Chelsea exclaimed as she looked at Tiffany.

"Woo hoo!" Tiffany raised her arms in triumph. "We're saved!"

Chelsea rubbed her hands together and looked-for closure. "So, Mr. private investigator – where do we go from here?"

Finn stroked his chin for a few seconds. "Actually, I have no idea what do to next."

"What?" the response came in stereo before Tiffany continued alone.

"What arrangements have you made?"

Finn shrugged and extended his arms to the side. "Arrangements? I haven't made any arrangements. I just have my friend waiting in a car outside on Morgan Avenue."

"Oh my God!" Chelsea buried her head in her hands. "Leave it to my mom to hire a moron for a private investigator."

"What does that mean?" Finn was instantly annoyed as Tiffany played peacemaker.

"Don't mind her. She' s got cabin fever from being cooped up in here for so long. Let's just stay with the current problem. What do we do now?"

Finn needed some plan to restore his image. "Why don't I drive you to your mom's place."

Chelsea's response did nothing for Finn's wounded image. "That's just great, Sherlock. And what do we do when those guys are there waiting for us? Instead of just me turning up dead, I'll have company at the funeral with Tiffany, my mom, and an imbecile private detective."

Finn realized his answer was indefensible, so he gritted his teeth and took it.

"Come on now." Tiffany clapped her hands. "We have to be able to think of some place we can go right now where it's safe, and this whole ordeal will be over."

Several seconds of silence indicated independent thought was taking place. Finn's private deliberations were interrupted by the vibrations of his iPhone.

"What's up, Kev?"

The rare sense of seriousness in Kevin's voice alerted Finn to a serious problem.

"Hey Finn – two cars just pulled up out here and there's five guys standing on the sidewalk near the entrance to this place."

"What do they look like?"

"Let's just say they ain't no Chinamen factory workers – and at least one of them is packing heat."

Even in this emerging crisis, Finn's first desire was the ability to reach through the phone, grab Kevin by the throat and shout, "Will you stop using these corny gun phrases!" Before Finn could say anything, however, Kevin was back on the air.

"Heads up, buddy. They're in the driveway heading your way. Be careful!"

Finn dropped the phone to his side. "They're here!"

Chelsea was beside herself. "You incredible asshole! You never checked to see if you were being followed?"

Finn ignored the rant and assumed the role of the adult in the room. "OK, we can't go out of here to the street. Too bad we can't untie this boat and make a water escape."

Before Chelsea could unload on Finn again, Tiffany chimed in. "Hey, we can't escape on the Sea Buddy, but there are other vessels."

"What do you mean?" Finn asked.

"The motorboats they used to use to get to Manhattan. They're still tied up off the stern."

Finn nodded in approval. "You know, that might just work. I've never been on Newtown Creek, but I do know that its channels feed out to New York Harbor and open water."

"Don't be ridiculous," Chelsea scoffed. Tiffany said those boats haven't been used in ages."

"Sounds like a plan," Finn stated with the satisfaction of finally being able to knock Chelsea down a notch.

Finn went into the passageway and peeked through a porthole toward the factory and the street. "I don't see them. They must be checking the factory. This is our chance – we have to go NOW!"

Finn went directly to the plank he had used to access the Sea Buddy, and reset it as a bridge. He followed Chelsea and Tiffany down the plank with the same technique he had used to board – quick, careful steps with eyes fixed straight ahead.

The boats were tied about six feet below the level of the dock, and a brand-new crisis erupted when Finn noticed all the rungs on the ladder attached to the dock were gone. Without a word of explanation Finn prostrated himself on the dirty gravel, his arms hanging over the edge of the dock.

"Come on ladies – quickly – climb over the edge of the dock and take my hands. I'll lower you to the boat."

After Tiffany was on board, it was much easier to lower Chelsea with Tiffany providing support from below. Before he released Chelsea's hands, Finn wondered if Chelsea would give him any credit for this idea. With both girls safely on board the small boat, it suddenly occurred to Finn that maybe his idea wasn't so wonderful. How was he going to get down to the boat?

There would be no accolades from Chelsea. "Come on! What are you waiting for?"

Finn made an about face and lowered himself over the edge of the dock, supporting himself on his elbows. Meanwhile, Chelsea continued her onslaught. "Will you come on. What are you going to do? – hang over the edge until they see you?"

Chelsea's verbal assault had the desired effect. Finn pushed off from the dock and fell backwards to the boat. He was only a couple of feet above the deck of the small vessel, and the girls were occupying most of the deck space, so he actually made a very soft-landing compliment of the bodies of Tiffany and Chelsea.

As they all lay on the aluminum deck, Tiffany laughed and sounded very much the thespian. "What a marvelous way to enter a scene."

Chelsea, on the other hand, was not amused. "Why didn't you warn us you were going to jump on us, you ass?"

Chelsea went directly to the bow and began unwinding the heavy rope from around the cleat. "I'll release the bow line, someone see if this motor works, or if we're going to have to row."

Finn was standing in the stern, directly adjacent to the outboard motor. He faced the motor and made numerous movements with his hands and arms, but in reality, he had absolutely no idea how to start that engine.

The newly untied vessel began to drift slightly from the dock as a frustrated Chelsea charged to the stern. "Get out of the way!" She demanded, brushing Finn aside with her right hand. Chelsea studied the motor and verbalized her assessment. "There's gas in it." She manipulated the choke for a few seconds before turning toward her crew. "Well, here goes nothing!"

Chelsea took a firm hold on the handle of the pull rope, took a last deep breath and yanked the handle as hard as she could. There was only the hint of a sputtering motor. She adjusted the choke again and pulled. The motor seemed a bit more alive, but it didn't turn over. After several additional unsuccessful attempts, Chelsea's labored breathing prompted Finn to offer support.

"Let me take over."

Chelsea's hand became an immediate stop sign. She drew in a deep breath and yanked the pull string again. The sputtering intensified until finally, the engine turned over. Tiffany was elated. "Great job girl! How do you know all this stuff?"

Chelsea needed a moment to regroup. She sat on the bench in the stern adjacent to the motor. "My dad had a boat like this when I was a little girl. We went out on it all the time."

Chelsea left no question as to who was the captain of this ship. "I'll navigate the rudder." She nodded toward Finn. "You do know how to get out of here, don't you?"

"Of course," Finn declared with confidence. He had taken enough abuse from this girl, so he certainly was not going to provide fodder for more criticism by showing any hesitation about his ability to direct them through Newtown Creek. Besides, as far as he knew, the creek only had one outlet – the harbor. If they simply followed the channels they would ultimately end up in the open water of the East River.

Chelsea continued her commands. "Get up in the bow and tell me how to steer."

Finn made another tactical error when he attempted to clarify nautical terms. "So, I just want to be clear. Which way is starboard and which way is port?"

Chelsea put her hand on her forehead and looked at Tiffany. "I don't believe this guy." She then redirected to Finn. "Just yell RIGHT or LEFT and point, genius!"

Chelsea throttled up the motor and steered the ten-foot aluminum watercraft into the middle of the creek. At this point, there was only one way to follow the channel, so Finn remained silent at the bow. He marveled at the size of this body of water. When he heard the term "Creek", Finn envisioned a babbling brook out in the country with ankle deep water flowing through the rocks. In the middle of Newtown Creek, he realized that this babbling brook had to be at least two hundred feet wide. Finn had no idea how deep the water was, but even if it was only waist deep, he was careful not to fall in. From the look of the heavily polluted water, Finn believed that a bath in this water would surely have consequences – perhaps the growth of a tail or at minimum the ability to glow in the dark.

Finn was beginning to feel upbeat. The short trip had so far been without incident as the boat sputtered under the Grand Street Bridge and followed the channel as it turned drastically to the east. The eastern path of the channel continued for about a half mile. Up ahead, Finn began to take notice of something that immediately placed a damper on his positive frame of mind. The channel was about to turn again, but this time a choice had to be made. The eastern path terminated, but it turned to both the north and south. Which direction led to the East River? Finn wasn't sure. Was it possible that both channels fed into the river? A decision had to be made, and as usual, a voice from the stern was about to force the issue.

"Well – which way?"

In the space of two seconds, Finn was about to say RIGHT, then changed to LEFT, but when his mouth opened it was RIGHT that provided the guidance for Chelsea.. Chelsea guided the boat onto its new southerly course, and the journey continued – hopefully to the open waters of the East River.

They passed under another bridge as the channel bent to the west before returning to its southern path. During the entire trip, the scenery on both sides of the creek was exclusively industrial ugliness, with junk yards, concrete plants and lumber yards lining the creek and competing for who had the least attractive location. As the boat made the westerly bend in the channel after the bridge, Finn took note of a break in the usual scenery. Off to the east was a very clean, modern looking facility that looked totally out of place in the industrial wasteland. Finn actually recognized the site. During his police academy training, he had received a class on the lesser known sensitive locations in the city, and he recognized this site as the Metropolitan Transportation Authority's Revenue Facility. This Fort Knox-like location was the depository for all the money coming in from New York City's subways, buses, railroads and bridges and tunnels. The facility looked like something of a fortress, and it was not well-publicized – the theory being that the less people who knew about a site on the Brooklyn / Queens border that had over three billion dollars in cash passing through it each year – the better.

Finn's trip down police academy memory lane was disrupted by a very angry sounding captain of the boat.

"Up ahead. Look!"

Finn immediately reacted to the voice and turned toward the stern to see Chelsea standing at the rudder, pointing toward the bow with her free hand. Finn turned back to view the southerly path of the boat, and instantly became aware of Chelsea's warning. The ten-foot high steel mesh and barb wire security fence of the Revenue Facility was to the east and the unattractive bulkhead and concrete wall of a lumber yard provided the border to the west. Dead ahead to the south, however, was Metropolitan Avenue, and there was no Metropolitan Avenue Bridge to pass under. This was a dead end.

Finn tried to beat Chelsea to the punch, with directions for a new course. He stammered as he attempted to come up with the proper nautical direction. "Uhhh…come….turn….oh hell – MAKE A U-TURN!"

Chelsea pulled the rudder hard right, but her navigation didn't stop her from unloading further on Finn. "You really know where you're going, don't you?" Chelsea scoffed.

Finn was really beginning to find Chelsea's sarcasm and comments ponderous, but he stayed focused on the problem at hand. "Just go back the way we came. That has to lead to the river."

"Duh! Ya think?"

Finn simply looked down to the deck and bit his lip. Maybe saving this girl was not such a great idea after all.

As the boat began turning into the bend, Tiffany was the first to see them. "Oh my God!"

Just beginning the bend in the channel about a quarter mile away were two other small motorboats. Chelsea was quick to jump on Finn. "I guess you never considered disabling the other two boats, did you?

Finn finally had enough. "Neither did you – now SHUT UP!"

Finn risked injuring his neck with the rate he was spinning his head to the right, left, and behind him. The prospects of a workable plan were not good. There was no way to get up to Metropolitan Avenue. To the west, the rotting wood bulk head and concrete wall prevented escape via the lumber yard, and to the east, the imposing security fence and barb wire of the MTA facility seemed impenetrable.

Suddenly, his head sprung back to the MTA facility. There was something that he saw when making the first pass by the site he needed to see again. Finn pointed to the two o'clock position. "Go right – quick – by those big rocks."

Chelsea complied without comment. As the boat drew closer to the eastern bank of the creek and a formation of large rocks, Finn shouted in triumph. "YES!"

What Finn had noticed during the first pass by was accurate. Just above the rocks was a break between the perimeter of the MTA site and the adjacent concrete plant to the north. As the boat approached the rocks Finn could see that there appeared to be at least a six-foot space between the MTA's security fence and the concrete plants concrete wall. He had no idea where the cavity between the two sites led to, but it was their only hope.

The bow hit one of the large rocks with a thud. Finn was quick to supply direction. "Out! Quick! Up the rocks!"

Finn's right knee buckled when he hopped out onto the lowest rock. Tiffany grabbed his hand as she landed on the same rock. "Are you OK?"

"Yeah, yeah," Finn grimaced. "We have to keep moving!"

Chelsea completed abandoning ship, settling on the adjacent rock. "Finally, some good advice," She lamented.

The first sound Finn heard was a whishing by his right ear. This was followed by the splashing water jumping up near the creek bank. The distant popping coming from the direction of the two boats emerging from around the bend confirmed the situation. Tiffany was first to react. Gone was the tone of an actor performing a classic on stage. At that moment her accent was all New York City. "Holy shit! They're shooting at us."

Finn was still in a seated position on the rock, making his hand's journey to his ankle quicker. Without using any of his police academy training regarding sight alignment and trigger control, Finn sprayed seven rounds from his 9mm pistol in the general direction of the two boats. Finn realized his shots came nowhere near his targets, but his fire had the desired effect when both boats temporarily veered off from their paths.

Finn thought about holstering his weapon back on his ankle, but stuck the gun inside his jacket pocket instead. He labored to his feet. "Let's move!" he shouted.

The path between the concrete plant wall and the MTA security fence was about six feet wide and was an uneven combination of uncut grass, weeds, dirt, and rocks of various sizes. The voluminous amount of CCTV cameras on top of the MTA fence provided Finn hope that someone might be watching their flight.

The "no-man's land" between the two facilities ran east for about a thousand feet before turning south. Finn knew instinctively that the turn would be the moment of truth. Would they be able to get out to civilization or would they face another dead-end.

As the trio traversed the uneven terrain as quickly as possible, Chelsea made an inquiry. "Are you empty?"

"What?" Finn puffed.

"Your gun – your gun!"

"I'm not sure – don't really know how many rounds I let go."

"Well, drop your mag and reload anyway," Chelsea directed.

"Reload?" Part of Finn's surprise was the realization that he wasn't carrying any extra magazines, but the other revelation was the reality that besides being nautically knowledgeable, Chelsea obviously knew about guns as well.

As they drew closer to the turn, Chelsea let loose with more frustration. "Don't tell me you're not carrying extra magazines. Please don't tell me that."

"OK, I won't tell you." Finn responded.

Finn ushered the girls into the turn and looked behind him before continuing. He could see the group of pursuers on the path, about seven hundred feet behind. As they ran south along the path, they passed two gates in the MTA fence – both locked. Additionally, the steel mesh material on the MTA security fence prevented visibility. There was no way to see what was on the other side of the fence.

The end of the road was upon them. The path terminated at one last gate. This was their last chance of escape. Finn reached for the gate first – Locked. Finn turned to face the pursuers, who had made the turn on the path and were cautiously approaching with weapons at the ready. In a chivalrous maneuver, Finn placed himself in front of the girls. Despite his gallantry, Chelsea continued to chide him. “What are you waiting for – Shoot!”

“I don’t even know if there are any rounds left.”

“Well, there’s only one way to find out, isn’t there?”

“No.” Finn sighed and raised his hands, accepting the inevitable.

“You Wuss!” moaned Chelsea.

As the group inched closer, Finn was able to get a better view of his pursuers. There were five of them, and as they drew still closer, he began to recognize familiar faces. Detective Delvecchio was in the lead, the barrel of his pistol seemingly trained directly between Finn’s eyes. Flanking Delvecchio was the fashion plate of IAB, Defama and Karpinski, the retired detective. Finn’s trip down memory lane was not complete, however, as rounding out the group were the two Middle Eastern men who had given Finn a beating on Cross Bay Blvd.

Delvecchio became the spokesman as the group came to within twenty feet of Finn and the two ladies. “Just keep your hands way up there and don’t do anything stupid.”

The crashes were almost simultaneous, resulting in a synchronized spin to the north by the entire group of five. Besides hearing the crashes, Finn was in a position to see the two locked gates on the MTA fence fly open, followed immediately by the arrival on the path of heavily armed men in tactical gear. Finn counted six of them, to be precise. They wore body armor and ballistic helmets. The two team members in the lead carried ballistic shields, and at least two of the following team members carried long guns – probably shotguns. There was no mystery who these saviors were. Their body armor, ballistic shields and helmets were labeled "MTA Security Force." Finn's hope had apparently become reality. Evidently, the CCTV cameras on the fence had been monitoring the pursuit, triggering the response of the MTA's armed security force.

The orders coming from behind the ballistic shields were clear and unambiguous – Drop the weapons and everyone lay face down on the ground with arms outstretched and palms up.

From his prostrate position, out of the corner of his eye Finn could detect a lone figure stepping out from behind the protective barrier of tactical personnel. This man in a white uniform shirt seemed immense, although from Finn's current position with his right cheek pressed into the dirt anyone would likely look tall. The white shirt said nothing, as all Finn could hear was the cracking of the dirt and rock with each careful step the security commander took among the prone prisoners. The cracking footsteps abruptly stopped, followed by the only words uttered by the commander.

"Tie em!"

The command prompted movement that Finn perceived was coming from all directions. Finn's arms were yanked behind his back and one quick zipping sound later his hands were immobilized. Without the benefit of visibility, Finn still knew what had just happened. His hands had been cuffed with flexi-cuffs or zip-ties, and from the additional zipping emanating from all around him, the girls and the pursuing crew had also been cuffed.

A strong hand grabbed Finn under his left arm and shoulder and yanked him to his feet. As the tactically attired MTA officer began a frisk, Finn quickly blurted the location of the pistol in his jacket pocket. A quick scan of the terrain revealed Chelsea and Tiffany being frisked by a female security officer while several tactically clad officers worked on the crew of five. Finn's mouth dropped open wider and wider as he observed the array of firepower being removed from the crew. Finn turned his head toward Chelsea. Even under these circumstances he would not miss an opportunity for retribution. "Hey! See that?" Finn said while nodding toward all the weapons. "This Wuss probably just saved your life." Finn turned away, but quickly realized he wasn't finished and returned his head toward Chelsea. "Again!"

Obviously, Chelsea needed to have the last word. "Even a broken clock is right twice a day."

Finn was at the rear of the single file line of prisoners escorted through one of the security fence gates. They were now in the MTA facility parking lot, and seemingly in a different world. Cars and trucks on Metropolitan Avenue crawled along at a snail's pace while curious MTA workers stood on the steps outside the building lobby trying to figure out what was going on.

Mixed in with the normal sounds of New York City traffic, Finn could make out distant sirens. The sirens were gaining in intensity as if someone were very slowly turning up the volume on a television. When the siren sounds seemed to reach a zenith, a visual signal joined in.

Blue and red flashing lights announced the arrival of three NYPD patrol cars into the MTA parking lot.

The white shirt MTA commander, apparently a man of few words, barked a command.

"Turn!"

Finn and the other prisoners turned to face the security fence. Finn heard car doors slamming, boots stomping, as well as the language of the police uniform – that squeaking, jingling, and knocking of keys, leather, and other gun belt gear that speaks loudly when a police officer runs. Voices were now audible, but Finn could not discern what was being said.

Once again, the same commander's voice issued direction.

"Turn!"

Finn performed an about face away from the fence and took in the scene. The MTA tactical force had been joined by at least eight uniformed NYPD officers. The white shirt MTA commander was in discussion with a uniformed NYPD Captain. Finn's initial perception was that this captain seemed very young for the rank – maybe mid-thirties at most. The young captain's eyes appeared extremely wide, like a deer caught in headlights. Finn feared this captain may be in over his head.

Finn had not seen the prelude to the current activity, but as he turned and assessed the scene , an NYPD cop was leading Delvecchio by the arm over to the Captain and the security commander. Thankfully, Finn was able to hear the next conversation. Delvecchio was running an incredible line of shit. In his story, the Intelligence Division was working on a highly sensitive and super-secret counterterrorism investigation in conjunction with the Department of Homeland Security. He directed the Captain to pull a piece of paper from his right pants pocket. Finn could see the Captain unfold a very official looking document. Delvecchio continued his tale by explaining that the form was a special federal warrant giving him the authority as a deputized US Marshal, to take custody of Finn and the girls. He continued to lay it on thick by emphasizing that national security interests were at stake, and that he could not divulge the location where he would take the detainees.

Chelsea and Tiffany could also hear the conversation. Tiffany commented with a degree of admiration. "That guy should be on stage. He's good."

Chelsea, on the other hand, chose to speak on her favorite topic. "Why don't you do something? You're just going to stand here and let them take us, you buffoon!"

Finn was into his "Names will never harm me" stage of dealing with Chelsea, so he chose to ignore her and continue focusing on the conversation.

Finn's spirits sank when the anxious Captain whispered in the MTA commander's ear, prompting the commander to order the flexi-cuffs cut off Delvecchio. Delvecchio and the Captain seemed like old friends now, as he rubbed his hands together to get the circulation going and continued to lay it on thick. He told the Captain that not many people realize there are black sites in the United States that officially don't exist, and that one of these non-locations was where he would be taking Finn and the girls. Finn was sure that the only black site he was destined for was six feet under, so he finally took Chelsea's advice.

"Excuse me, Captain – Please, I have to talk to you."

The young Captain took one step toward Finn, but Delvecchio cut him off at the pass.

"Sorry Captain, all conversations with these detainees are now classified as national security issues. I can't stop you from talking to him, but if you choose to continue, you will have to appear tomorrow morning before a judge at the Second Circuit Southern District Federal Court in Manhattan to show cause that your conversations were necessary."

The Captain advanced no further, invoking Delvecchio's gratitude.

"Thank you, sir."

The Captain turned to the MTA commander. "Give them back their weapons, and my people will escort them off the property." The Captain turned back to Delvecchio. "Do you need any further assistance?"

"We could use some help, Cap." Delvecchio responded. "These guys gave us quite a chase. Can we get a ride back to our vehicles on Morgan Avenue?"

"No problem, Detective." The Captain seemed relieved that the incident appeared to be settled.

There was no more edge to Chelsea's voice. Her tone was now one of accepting the inevitable. "We are truly fucked!"

"Here, Here!" lauded Tiffany.

Displays of mutual gratitude were expressed between the NYPD and the MTA security force as Delvecchio grabbed Finn by his left arm and began leading him across the parking lot. Karpinski and Defama led the way, both with firm grips on Tiffany and Chelsea.

Approximately fifty feet from the patrol car that would transport them back to Morgan Avenue, Finn began to hear a familiar sound. It was that same sound from minutes earlier – the distant siren getting progressively louder and louder. A dark Chevy Caprice flew through the parking lot gate, siren blaring with the accompanying portable red light rotating on the dashboard inside the front windshield.

Finn spoke to himself in a low tone. "Finally!"

The Caprice screeched to a stop, cutting off the entourage from their vehicles. The front passenger door swung open and out stepped a uniformed NYPD Deputy Chief.

"I'm taking command of this incident." The words were spoken by NYPD Deputy Chief Patrick Delaney.

Delvecchio was still a very cool customer. He maintained his firm grip on Finn as he walked him towards Patrick Delaney. He produced his bogus warrant again for additional effect.

"Everything's under control, Chief. We got this." Delvecchio cheerfully stated.

The captain chimed in to reassure Chief Delaney. "It's OK, Chief – it's a federal thing – top secret, but I took care of it.."

Finn was no more than six feet from his dad as Delvecchio extended the phony warrant towards the Chief. Finn locked eyes with his father, and when he was sure he had his attention, he silently mouthed one deliberate word – "GUNS!"

Finn thought he detected a slight nod of acknowledgement from his dad, but that may have been wishful thinking. Patrick took the warrant and summoned the Captain and the MTA commander into a private huddle about twenty feet from Finn and Delvecchio. The huddle broke and Patrick carefully folded the paper and extended it to Delvecchio.

"Thanks, Chief." Delvecchio smiled.

Patrick returned the smile, leaned in close to Delvecchio's right ear and whispered, "You're done.

"On the ground – now – all of you!"

The bellowed command came from the MTA security commander, who apparently had a few more words in him. The MTA tactical team, backed up by the NYPD contingent, initiated a tactical approach behind their ballistic shields.

In the end, Delvecchio and his crew went down quickly and without a fight. Chief Delaney left the freshly overwhelmed Captain to sort out the remainder of the incident while he quickly ushered Finn and the girls into the back of his Caprice.

Finn slid into the back seat between Tiffany and Chelsea. Patrick settled into the front passenger seat and addressed his driver. "Let's go Jack."

"Which way Chief?" the driver inquired.

Patrick shifted in the seat and looked back. "Which way Finneous?"

Finn was unclear of the next step. "Where are we going?"

Patrick raised his eyebrows. "We're taking this young lady home, of course."

"Oh!" Finn mumbled.

Patrick pointed to his driver. "Tell Jack which way to go."

Finn leaned forward. “Left on Metro – then go to Woodhaven and make a right.”

“Got it,” Jack responded as the Caprice made a left out of the MTA parking lot.

Finn sat back and took a deep breath, his body finally relaxing. Chelsea must have realized that it had been at least five minutes since she last insulted Finn. “You have to excuse him sir,” she stated to Patrick. “He’s somewhat dense.”

Patrick turned in his seat and chuckled. “Somewhat dense? Sometimes he’s just plain dumb.”

Chelsea shrieked with delight at finding a new ally. Finn was too spent to get excited anymore. All he could do is close his eyes and muster a weak protest. “Don’t you start on me too, dad.”

Chelsea stopped laughing and spun her head toward Finn and then back to Patrick. “You’re his father?” Chelsea questioned.

“That’ s right, young lady. Fineous can be a real imbecile at times, but he also just saved your life.”

Chelsea and Tiffany both leaned forward in their seats, but remained silent as Patrick explained. “Sometime during your chase, Finn was able to 911 text me, and I just used the phone tracking feature in his iPhone to find you guys.”

“You cut it a little close, didn’t you dad?” Finn declared.

“Hey Fineous, I was in the war room at headquarters in a CompStat crime statistics meeting. When your text came in I just ran out of One Police Plaza without explanation.”

Woodhaven Blvd. had turned into Cross Bay Blvd. Chelsea leaned forward and provided Jack the final instructions. "A couple of more blocks ahead – 12th Street – make a right.'

The red light was still revolving on the dashboard when Jack pulled to a stop in front of the tiny bungalow. Finn could see Susan in the living room window. She had the anguished look of a mother expecting the worst news from an arriving police vehicle. Finn observed the look transition to total relief as Chelsea emerged from the back seat. By the time Finn and Tiffany were on the sidewalk, Susan Garland had charged out the front door and front gate. The emotional reunion made Finn feel good. Tiffany tapped Finn's shoulder and pointed toward Cross bay Blvd. "Hey, there's my old stomping ground. I played my best role there."

"You sure did." Finn smiled.

Susan was still gushing with emotion, but she also was trying to maintain her social graces. "Please, everyone – come in for coffee and cake. I won't take no for an answer."

Patrick looked to the Caprice. "Lock it up, Jack and come on in."

Susan ushered Patrick, Jack, and Tiffany through the front door. Chelsea motioned for her mother to go ahead. "I'll be right in, mom."

With Susan in the house, Chelsea turned on the top step and virtually leaped into Finn's arms. Her emotions were still flowing as freely as her tears. She released new tears into Finn's right shoulder before drawing back and looking directly into his eyes. "I'm so sorry for everything I said. I owe you everything." Chelsea leaned forward and kissed Finn on his left cheek. She resumed eye contact, and slowly, a smile began to emerge until it was a wide grin. "But you're still a lousy private detective." Chelsea let out a hearty laugh, but Finn's laugh was just a little louder.

Finn was still chuckling as he guided Chelsea through the front door. "Let's see if you mom's coffee is as good as Kevin's."

Chelsea turned in the doorway. "Who's Kevin?"

"Oh shit! I forgot about him." Finn raised the index finger of his right hand indicating he would be delayed.

"I'll be right in," He said to Chelsea as he retreated to the stoop, iPhone already at his ear.

Kevin's patience had apparently drained. "Well, it's about time. What the hell are you doing in there? And where are those guys? I gotta tell you, Finbar, I was about ready to go home."

Finn chuckled. "That's a good idea Kev – go home and I'll get the car tomorrow."

"What?"

"I'll explain tomorrow – no, I'm gonna need some time to unwind. I'll see you when I see you."

With his phone back in his pocket, Finn was again through the doorway. "Now, let's see how good this coffee is."

THE GREATEST COUNTRY IN THE WORLD

DECEMBER 31st - Finn pushed open the heavy oak door and entered his comfort zone – the dark, empty world of the Shamrock Bar.

"Well, well – Look whose back among the living." Kevin came out from behind the bar and completed the manly hug ritual.

Finn settled in on a stool. "I needed some time to recharge the batteries, but today, I just had to have a cup of your coffee."

"Coming up, bro," Kevin returned behind the bar and went to work. "I read some wild shit in the papers about everything that went down."

"That's not the half of it." Finn responded.

Kevin poured two cups of coffee. He graciously held the bottle of Bailey's up for Finn to decline before spiking his own cup. "Cheers, my friend!" The two cups clinked loudly when they met.

Finn took his first sip and placed his cup on the bar. "Mmm…You may not be good for much, but you can sure make a great cup of coffee. Are you working tonight?"

"Well thank you, Finbar. That's probably the nicest thing you've ever said to me, and yes, I am working. It will be three deep at the bar tonight." Kevin sampled his own spiked coffee. He then came out from behind the bar and took the stool next to Finn. "So, tell me, what was the real story with these mopes who tried to off you."

"Off me?" Finn didn't have the energy to deal with Kevin's corny slang jargon.

"Yeah. All those guys with the gats."

Finn slowly turned on the stool to face Kevin, totally ignoring another ridiculous gun reference. "Well, I guess I should start with exactly what was going on the night Chelsea got in trouble. The crown prince of Bahrain was out on the town with his private security detail.

"Crown prince of where?" Kevin interrupted.

"Bahrain," Finn responded before quickly remembering his friend's mental limitations. "Brains…you remember…the King of Brains?"

"Oh yeah – the King of Brains – I remember."

With his friend now clarified, Finn continued. "The prince was following his standard script – trolling Manhattan clubs for women. So, the entourage visits the Carleton Club in Midtown, and the prince goes directly into a private VIP suite. By this time, his flunkies know the drill and they know exactly the type of women the prince likes, so Delvecchio begins circulating in the bar looking for pretty girls who want to attend the prince's private party. The first girl Delvecchio worked his magic on was poor Cynthia Dubois. Delvecchio had enough experience doing this that he knew the prince needed more than one girl, so he basically drops Cynthia off at the door to the suite and returns to the bar for more prey. "

"This is when he found Chelsea?" Kevin interjected.

Finn was actually surprised. "That's right. You really may not be as dumb as you appear to be."

Kevin chuckled. "That may well be the second nicest thing you've ever said to me."

"Well, anyway," Finn continued. "Delvecchio runs his line of shit on Chelsea and begins to walk her to the suite. Meanwhile, the prince is not wasting anytime.

Evidently. As soon as he is introduced to Cynthia, he drops his pants in the middle of the room."

"Oh my God! What did she do?" Kevin asked.

"She laughed." Finn answered.

"Size?" Kevin laughed.

"Maybe." Finn was not laughing. "Anyway, when Cynthia laughs in his face, the prince reaches back and backhands her across her face. She loses her balance, falls backwards and hits her head on the edge of a table. That's it – that's the whole story. Cynthia Dubois died because she laughed at that asshole prince."

"But he didn't mean to kill her. Why didn't they just report it?"

"Who knows?" Finn stated. "Maybe they didn't want an international incident or anything to disrupt the Bahrainian Motors auto plants that were coming here. Maybe the prince just felt he should be immune from any legal scrutiny."

"But what about the cops?"

Finn knew exactly what Kevin meant. "You underestimate the power of greed, my friend. Delvecchio, Karpinski, and Defama had long ago sold their loyalty to this guy because of the extravagant tips they received. When the shit hit the fan, their entire mission became keeping the prince out of this mess. They put two .22 slugs in the girl's head and threw her in the dumpster. Then, they find this homeless zombie who doesn't even know what year it is. They put the murder weapon in his hand, have him sign a confession, and arrange for his suicide. All the loose ends were tied up into one nice neat little package. But they still had one problem to deal with – Chelsea Garland."

"Money." Kevin shook his head. I guess I'm better off without it.

"You may be right. Look what it did to those cops. They were actually willing to commit murder to keep their cash faucet turned on."

"So, what actually happened to all these guys" Kevin asked.

"Delvecchio, Defama, and Karpinski were charged with everything but the kitchen sink – murder, attempted murder, assault, reckless endangerment and a lot more I can't even remember right now. They'll probably cop a plea at some point to lesser charges – but they're going inside – that's for sure."

"And the brains guys?" Kevin followed up.

Finn snickered. "Nothing!"

"What?"

"The prince and the two security agents that tuned me up had diplomatic immunity. All that could be done was to toss them all back to Bahrain. Apparently, however, our warm fuzzy relationship with Bahrain is history – at least for now – and that deal for the auto plants is done before it ever started.

Finn polished off the last of his coffee. "You know who the biggest loser is in this whole caper?"

"Who?" Kevin asked.

"The poor guy who ends up marrying that girl Chelsea. What a handful she is. Her mom said she was smart, but she forgot one important word. In all my life I never met a more sarcastic smart ASS."

Kevin slapped the bar and howled in delight. "That line, my pal, deserves a toast – a real toast."

Kevin grabbed two shot glasses and plunked them on the bar. He quickly poured two shots of Sambuca with the skill of an experienced bartender. Finn decided to honor this toast and raised his glass. Kevin began to do the same but stopped. A wide grin emerged on his face. "Hey Meg, come here and join the party."

"Oh, hey Finn. I didn't see you come in." Meg joined the duo at the bar.

"Join us Meg?" Kevin slid a shot glass in front of Meg.

"No, no, no!" Meg waved off the drink. "It's going to be a long day and night. If I start drinking now I'll never make it to the new year."

"Well then," Kevin raised his glass. "Here's to us, Finbar!"

"To us!" Finn met the other glass with a loud clink.

The toast completed, Kevin remembered he actually had to work. "I gotta go downstairs and bring up supplies. Do me a favor and keep your eye on the door – it's open."

"Sure thing, barkeep." Finn had not taken a shot in a long time, and the Sambuca was going right to his head.

"So, what are you doing tonight?" Meg asked.

"Tonight?" Finn was confused.

"Yeah, tonight," Meg repeated.

"What's tonight?"

"New Year's silly!" Meg laughed.

With everything that had occurred plus the addition of the Sambuca, the new year had slipped out of Finn's consciousness. "Oh yeah! Not much. I'm not doing anything."

"Why don't you come by here and keep me company."

"I don't know…I guess…maybe." Finn was blowing it again, and the worst part was he knew it, but he couldn't stop himself.

Thankfully, Meghan provided one more chance. "Well, if you are available I can't think of anyone else I would rather ring in the new year with."

Finn smiled. He would sabotage himself no more. Finn took Meg's hand. "And there is no one I would rather be with on New Year's Day - or any day. I'll be here." Finn squeezed Meg's hand tighter. The discomfort was obvious, but he needed to finally get this off his chest. "Meg, I'm so sorry for.."

Finn's apology was halted by Meg's index finger on his lip. "Shhsh…Don't!" She smiled warmly while backing away. "I'll see you later."

"It's a date!" Finn called out.

"A date?" Kevin had just returned behind the bar. "What's this I'm hearing about a date?"

"That's right! A date!" Finn grinned defiantly.

"Well, it's about time." Kevin responded. "I was beginning to have serious doubts about you, Finbar." Never one to miss an opportunity to drink, Kevin discovered the subject for a new toast. He filled the shot glasses and raised his glass. "To our friend, Meg!"

"What the hell!" Finn raised his glass. "To Meg!"

Both glasses plopped down on the bar. "That will grow some hair on you." Kevin remarked. Finn stared out the window to Woodhaven Blvd. which was now beginning to spin slightly. Kevin's voice brought Finn's attention back to the bar.

"Oh, by the way. You do realize that I got screwed in this incident, don't you?"

"How's that?" Finn was legitimately confused.

"The prince of brains car – the Mansour. I had a pre-order in, and now that's completely out the window."

Finn thought the shots were affecting his hearing. "Now wait a minute. I know exactly what the price of that car was going to be – 70K!"

"So?" Kevin asked incredulously.

"So, how the hell did you get financing on a seventy-thousand-dollar car. This job isn't even on the books. You have no reported income. How in God's name is that possible?"

Kevin smiled. "Because," he pointed to the American Flag on a stick proudly protruding from the top of an empty Sambuca bottle on the top shelf of the bar, "this is America – the greatest country in the world."

Finn returned the smile and raised his freshly refilled glass. "To America!"

About the Author

Robert L. Bryan is a law enforcement and security professional. He served twenty years with the New York City Transit Police and the New York City Police Department, retiring at the rank of Captain. Presently, Mr. Bryan is the Chief Security Officer for a New York State government agency. He has a B.S in criminal justice from St. John's University and an M.S. in security management from John Jay College of Criminal Justice. Additionally, Mr. Bryan is an Adjunct Professor in the Homeland Security Department and the Security Systems and Law Enforcement Technology Department for two New York Metropolitan area colleges. For more information about Mr. Bryan's other books, please visit his website: www.robertbryanauthor.com

Made in the USA
Las Vegas, NV
20 October 2021

32737854R00121